# Berlin Blind ·

# Berlin Blind

## Alan Scholefield

HEINEMANN : LONDON

William Heinemann Ltd
10 Upper Grosvenor Street, London W1X 9PA

LONDON MELBOURNE TORONTO
JOHANNESBURG AUCKLAND

First published 1980

434 67860 0

Set, printed and bound in Great Britain by
Fakenham Press Limited, Fakenham, Norfolk

"It appears that of the hundreds of thousands of prisoners of war in Germany only thirty-odd volunteered for the corps (the British Free Corps). But even so small a number, split into groups and sent into the German towns, drunken and with prostitutes on their arms, did something to raise national morale . . ."

*     *     *

"There were also the children among the traitors, the ones who thought like children, and felt like children, and were treacherous as children are, without malice . . . most of these were children with men's bodies; but some were children in body as well as mind."

Rebecca West, *The Meaning of Treason.*

For Hugh Toomer

# London

## PART I

A little before full dark on an early autumn evening in London a Volkswagen microbus with German tourist plates pulled off the carriageway in Hyde Park and stopped in the deserted parking area overlooking the Serpentine. Two men sat in the front seat. The driver was twenty-eight years old, a big man who wore a heavy black beard and long hair. He was dressed in jeans, a white T-shirt, and a camouflage jacket; on his feet he wore Adidas running shoes. His name was Jurgen Muller and he had been born in Hanover in West Germany. He sat for some moments, his big hands resting on top of the steering-wheel, and stared out over the darkling water; then he looked at his watch and said to his companion: "He'll be late tonight."

The second man was shorter, with a nervous face, darting eyes and a moustache. His name was Louis Tellier, he was four years older than Muller, and had been born in Lyons. He wore dark grey pin-cords, a green polo-neck and, like his companion, Adidas running shoes. He had a mountaineer's beanie on his head.

"What time is it?" he said in English, their only common language.

"Nearly half-past."

"Did Inge phone?"

"An hour ago."

"And?"

"Everything under control."

A light drizzle began to fall, sweeping across the park from the north-east. It was not much more than a heavy mist but soon the beech trees and horse-chestnuts—already losing their leaves—began to glisten in the light from the lamps on the Serpentine bridge. The rain was not heavy enough to pucker

1

the surface of the water and the lake shone like a black-lacquered road that ended in the misty cliffs of Park Lane.

Tellier rolled down his window and held his hand out into the night, feeling the drizzle.

"Do you think he will come?"

"He'll come."

"Not if it is wet."

"I know him better than you."

Tellier looked at his watch. "How long do you think?"

"Half an hour. Perhaps a little more."

"You saw him go into the hotel?"

"I was parked across the street." For the first time a note of impatience entered Muller's voice. "Don't worry, he never misses. I've seen him go out in a thunderstorm. He'll come."

They sat in silence for a while then Tellier said, "Do you think he knows?"

"About us? Never."

"Sometimes I have the feeling . . . he went to the newspaper library at Colin-dale." He pronounced it carefully as two words.

"I know. So?"

"He looked back. Two times, three times."

"In the street?"

"Yes."

"You didn't go into the library?"

"No  But maybe he see me in the street?"

"You were on the other side?"

"A hundred metres away, almost."

"Your own mother wouldn't recognize you with a moustache and that thing on your head."

"You do not like it?"

"A cap, a hat, something to cover your head. No one talked of mountain-climbing."

"I did not have a hat."

"Christ, man, there are shops."

"The English wear these." Tellier took off the beanie, examined it, and pulled it on again. Without it he was completely bald. "He did not seem strange to you?"

2

"Normal. Everything the same. He went to Scotland Yard again. For more than an hour. A meeting, I suppose. Then I picked him up. Taxi to Kensing-ton"—he, too, split the word—"and here we are. We wait."

"Why does it have to be this way?"

"Which way?"

"Like this, in the park. All dressed up."

"You want to go up to him in the street. 'Good day, Herr Riemeck . . .' Is that your way?"

"His hotel room."

"The noise, Tellier, the noise. Anyway, what if he recognized us? He's a professional, you know. It is better in the dark. I'm glad it's raining. Look around you, No one."

Again there was a pause, then Tellier said, "Shouldn't we get ready?"

Muller looked at his watch. "All right."

They got out, opened the vehicle's wide side doors and climbed into the roomy interior. It was fitted up as a camper and there were two high-back seats facing each other like a booth in a bar. There was also a small wardrobe, a gas stove, a cupboard, and space for a table. From the wardrobe Muller took two coat-hangers; each held a dark-coloured track-suit. They began to change into them.

*　　*　　*

Less than twenty miles away at London Airport the drizzle had stopped and the big lights shone down on the glistening black tarmac. Inside Terminal Three it was impossible to tell whether it was day or night, wet or dry. Luggage from the New York Jumbo that had landed twenty minutes before was beginning to come down on Carousel Two and the passengers moved closer. John Spencer had gone off to get a trolley, and now, as the suitcases began to tumble down the chute he pushed forward, finding a way between the others, so that soon he was standing next to the Carousel itself. One or two people had turned round with irritation as the trolley brushed their legs and had seen a man of medium height, strongly built, with dark hair beginning to turn grey except for a line of white above one ear, and cold blue eyes. His hands on the trolley were blunt, square and powerful and he had an air of authority. He was completely unaware of the irritation he had caused. His mind was already probing at the hour that lay ahead: the car journey along the motorway then fighting the last of the rush-hour traffic through central London until finally he reached Hampstead and Sue. He wanted to see her so badly he could almost smell her and taste her.

His suitcase was one of the first to come down and he caught it up and put it on the trolley with his executive case, his coat and the plastic bag with the two half bottles of Remy Martin and the ounce of Miss Dior he had bought on the plane.

"Excuse me," he said and pushed his way through towards the green customs exit.

Robert Calland was waiting for him in the arrivals hall.

"Hello, John. Good to have you back."

"Hello, Bob." They shook hands. "Let's get the hell out of here. Where's the car?"

"Out front. Let me take that."

"No I can manage." He picked up the suitcase and strode off across the hall to the glass exit doors. Armstrong had the Mercedes half over a pedestrian crossing and a policeman was making his way towards them. Spencer threw his suitcase into the trunk, slammed it shut, and they took off hurriedly into the traffic.

"Good trip?" Calland said.

"So, so. I think we've got the Goddard contract."

"God, that's marvellous. Do you mean exclusively?"

"Yes. Not only for Britain but France and Belgium as well. I tried to get Holland but no dice."

"But that's great, John. It's more than we hoped for."

"It may have been more than you hoped for but I'd have liked Holland."

"Greedy."

Spencer smiled. In spite of the chilly blue eyes the smile had warmth. It gave him a boyish, youthful look. He knew it and used it to his advantage whenever he could.

They left the airport lights behind and swung out onto the

motorway. "That must have taken some talking," Calland said.

Spencer looked sideways at him under his eyelids. Calland was a good-looking young man on the way up and Spencer was never quite certain whether there wasn't a bit too much of the yes-man about him. He agreed with a lot of Spencer's thinking but then as Spencer had said to himself that might just be good sense. He was pushy and sometimes just a little too familiar. But Spencer did not mind. Calland was what, twenty-seven, twenty-eight, and Spencer had been as pushy, as ambitious at that age. Just as long as he didn't think he could trample on John Spencer.

"What do we pay?" Calland said.

"That's the part we haven't ironed out yet. They want six, I offered four, six if we got Holland."

"What are they like?"

"Pretty hard. Typical American business men." He thought of the big glass office in downtown Houston where they had had their meetings. There were none of the liquid lunches that the same sort of business discussion would have meant in London. There they worked in their shirt sleeves starting at eight in the morning, and some of them did not knock off until seven or eight in the evening. It was a sandwich and a glass of milk for lunch. Of course in the evening it had been different; then there had been the booze and the girls and he'd had his share of the booze but he had not been interested in the girls and he'd gone back to his room in the Ramada Inn near the Six-ten Loop, where he was staying so he could be close to the factory, and the first thing he'd done every evening was to phone Sue.

He'd only gone out twice during his fortnight in Houston, once to old man Goddard's mansion in River Oaks where there had been a black butler and three black maids serving at table, and the second time to Quail Valley to the home of a young executive about Calland's age where the houses were all grouped round a golf course and you took your martinis in a basket and put them on the golf cart; eighteen holes on a Sunday morning had very little to do with healthy exercise.

5

They were running into London now and the traffic was getting heavier. "Tell me about Metcalfe," Spencer said.

Calland looked away and then shrugged slightly. "No change."

"Well that's it then."

"He's good."

"Yes I know he's good."

Metcalfe was the new works manager at the factory in Slough where they made pressure valves of all kinds. Spencer had taken him off the shop floor and brought him up through the ranks of middle management. But his new position seemed to have gone to his head. He'd bought a second-hand Jaguar and for the past two months had been coming in late and leaving early. Spencer had spoken to Metcalfe about it and had asked Calland to reinforce the warning. It obviously hadn't worked and now they'd have to get rid of Metcalfe. "Oh, shit," he said. "I don't want to talk about it, I don't want to think about it." Armstrong was taking them through the backstreets, threading their way between the traffic jams towards north London.

"Did you see Susan?" Spencer said.

"We had her to dinner twice."

"That was kind of you."

"It was our pleasure, you know how Joan likes her. Then on Sunday we went down to Brighton for the day."

"Brighton?"

"Well it was sunny and Sue said she felt like a breath of sea air. Anyway, I like Brighton."

Spencer nodded. "Thanks, Bob. It took a load off my mind. How did you think she was looking?"

"Marvellous. You know what they say about pregnant women."

Armstrong drove Spencer to work every day and knew the by-ways of Belsize Park and Hampstead like a map and soon he was drawing up before one of the houses in Cannon Place. For the past five minutes Spencer had been wondering whether he could let Calland go without offering him a drink and had decided he couldn't. "Are you coming in for a quick one?"

"Thanks John, some other time."

Spencer could have kissed him. "O.K., Bob, I'll see you first thing in the morning and give you a run down on the whole operation."

He stood on the pavement and watched the car disappear down the short street and then he picked up his suitcase and walked through the garden gate and up the steps to the front door. He felt excited, like a kid. Sue's light was on and he wanted to shout or throw a stone against her window, but instead he gave three short rings on the bell. The door opened almost immediately and there she was standing in the hall with her arms outstretched to greet him, the great bulge of her belly threatening to pull her off balance.

"Darling. Darling. Darling," she said and put her arms round his neck and pulled him towards her.

"Careful," he said, breaking free after some moments. "You'll squeeze what's its name." He patted her tummy. "God it's good to see you."

"I heard the car. I came down. I knew you'd ring."

He left his suitcase in the hall and put his arm round her waist and they went into the drawing-room. There she turned and kissed him again. "It's been so *long*," she said. "The longest two weeks I've ever known."

She pushed him down onto the big sofa. "Sit. You must be tired. I'll get you a drink."

He watched her mix the Scotch and water and put in the ice. Everything had been ready for his homecoming. His mind went back to other trips and other years before his first wife Margaret had died. Things had been very different then, specially the last years. Then she would have been up in her own room and the only Scotch available would have been in the bottle she was drinking from. In those days he had spent as much time away from home as he could; he'd had no urge to get back. Business trips had been spun out long beyond their usefulness. He had looked forward to leaving and been depressed about returning. Now things were different; now Calland was taking over more and more on the foreign side and

Spencer was only doing the major trips; no more than two or three a year.

He looked at Susan. Calland was right, she was looking marvellous. She was a tall woman, about Spencer's own height with dark hair and a pale oval face. Normally she would have had slight hollows in her cheeks—she was on the thin side—but she had put on weight and her face had filled out and Spencer thought he had never seen her looking so beautiful. She was thirty-one, just over twenty years younger than Spencer, yet her skin was unlined and as fresh as it had been at twenty-five. She was wearing a long black kaftan with a chunky gold chain round her neck, gold earrings, and heavy gold dress rings on both her hands. He thought she looked exotic, Italianate. He told himself: "She's yours, she's your wife. Remember this moment. Remember how happy you are."

She poured herself a glass of tonic water—she was off alcohol now because of the baby—and sat beside him. "Tell me about it. But first, did you miss me?"

He took her hand and brought it up to his lips. "Every single minute of every day."

"I bet you didn't. What about these blonde bombshells that business men are supposed to organize on their trips abroad?"

"Oh, those. I had lots of those. I still missed you."

She laughed. "Why, what have I got that they haven't got?"

"Your figure." He patted her tummy again. "I've got used to ladies with large tummies."

They talked for a while and he told her about the trip and she told him how she had been and about her blood-pressure— up slightly—and how she had been out to dinner twice with the Callands and down to Brighton, and then she said, "How do you fancy a steak and a bottle of burgundy?"

"Couldn't be better. I'm up to here with tacos and enchiladas and hamburgers and things called chicken-fried steaks—"

"What on earth are those?"

"God knows, some sort of ground meat. They grind up everything in America. I asked for a wiener schnitzel one night and that was ground up too. But first of all a shower."

"And another drink?"

8

"Of course. Don't forget I'm drinking for three of us now."

"I'll bring it up."

He went upstairs and had his shower and came into the bedroom towelling himself. She was sitting on the edge of the bed holding his whisky. He took it from her and bent to kiss her forehead and she put her arms up and pulled him down beside her. She kissed him and this time there were both affection and passion in it.

"Now?" he said.

"Yes, now."

She unzipped the kaftan and took it off and she was wearing nothing underneath it. She lay on her side next to him propping her head up on her hand and he thought she looked like a piece of modern sculpture, all convoluted rounds and curves. Her breasts had enlarged and her nipples were a deep pink. Blue veins stood out both on her breasts and on her stomach, and her navel had inverted. He bent and kissed her stomach. This was one of the wonders of Susan, that throughout her pregnancy she had felt the physical need of sex. It had been quite the opposite with Margaret. She had felt ill for a lot of the time and perhaps because subconsciously she blamed sex for feeling so wretched, had grown to think of it with distaste, a distaste which had lasted for several months after the birth of their son, Dick.

He held Sue in his arms now and kissed her and they moved easily to a position where she lay half on top of him so that the pressure on her stomach was lessened. After it was over he lay in the softly lit room by her side, drowsy and content, as though suspended in time and space, weightless.

"How do you feel?" Sue said.

"As though I'm floating."

She took his arm and put it under her neck so that she could put her head on his chest. "Aren't we lucky?" she said.

"Touch wood."

His free hand stretched out and touched the wooden bedside table. Lucky. It was too small a word, too weak a word to describe his situation. Long ago with Margaret he had learned that happiness consisted of a series of negatives: it was not being ill, not having a row, not having a disaster at the factory. He imagined that when he had married Margaret he had been happy, or when Dick was born, and there must have been times when Dick was growing up that they'd been happy together. Or when his grandson was born. Or when he'd had success in business. But he could not remember those times. Now happiness was an almost tangible thing. It was being with Susan, it was enjoying what she called their luck. Here he was at fifty-two, when most men are levelling out, perhaps over the top, some with grandchildren, here he was with a young and beautiful wife who seemed to love him as much as he loved her, with a business that was booming, with a house in Hampstead, with all the good things of life at his fingertips. That was why he sometimes felt frightened. It was too good. A slight irritation came over him. It wasn't just luck. That assumed a passive role and long ago, long before he had met Susan and long before he had met Margaret he had learned how dangerous that could be. You had to grab life with both hands and force it to go your way otherwise it sucked you along like a blown leaf and then all you had to depend on was luck. No, he'd worked hard in more ways than one for what he had got, it wasn't simply luck.

Sue groaned lightly and he realized she must have drifted into sleep. The baby was due in just over a month and she often had spells of drowsiness followed by bursts of activity. Gently he raised her head and slipped out from under it. He covered her with the eiderdown and quietly went into his dressing-room. He put on a pair of corduroys, a thick plaid shirt and a pair of soft moccasins, went downstairs, made himself a fresh drink, and took it to his study on the first floor.

The house which was detached and stood in its own garden faced onto the small road, but the rear windows looked out over London from almost the top of Hampstead Hill. Because of the view Spencer had placed his desk directly in front of the window. He loved this room and spent a great deal of time in it when he was at home. Many an evening when he had work to do, he would sit at the desk and Sue would curl up on the big leather Chesterfield with a book.

10

He had lavished a great deal of money on the room. The carpet was heavy brown Wilton, the desk of English yew with a green leather top and a tooling of gold fleurs-de-lys. One wall was covered in books from floor to ceiling, a second had been designed for his stereo equipment: his big Tandberg reel-to-reel, his Grundig TV with video recorder, his Sony 32-band global radio. To the left of his stereo equipment were his two Nikon cameras with their series of wide-angle and telephoto lenses. Once, in the last years with Margaret, these technological toys had been his life-line, now he hardly touched them.

In those days he had practically lived in his study, while Margaret had had the room directly above him as her sitting-room. Every night, as he worked on his papers, he would hear her crossing the floor to her bathroom to fetch water for her whisky. He could tell the number of drinks she'd had by the amount of walking she did. Some nights he would hear her cross the floor eight or ten times, on others five or six and then there would be silence and he knew she would be asleep in her chair or in a heap on her bed. Sometimes she fell—a crash over his head as he worked—and he would go upstairs and find her in a state of drunken collapse and he would have to put her to bed. He hated that part, he hated undressing her.

They had lived a strange life, just the two of them in the big house, he with his work, she with her half-read books and magazines, her TV set, her bottles. In the old days the house had been filled with people. They had employed a cook, a Portuguese maid and a chauffeur. But when Margaret had started drinking things had changed. First the maid had gone because she refused to clean up the physical mess left by his wife, and then the cook had given notice because everything she made was returned uneaten. The chauffeur, Armstrong, still drove him back and forth to the office but he was a company employee and had nothing to do with the household.

It was not always the same. Sometimes Margaret would seem to recover for several days at a time, not totally, she was always slightly drunk, but enough to get him his dinner when he came home in the evening; enough to pretend that they were maintaining some vestige of ordinary life. They might even go out together to a theatre or a movie. Soon after Margaret started drinking in earnest they no longer went to friends, there were too many disasters in other people's houses. After a while they had dropped out of touch with the few friends they had made.

Spencer remembered once during a "normal" period he had bought a Morgan sports car and had taken her for a drive in it, up through Golders Green and Hendon and onto the M1 as far as Baldock and back. She had endured the hard springing and noise and the cutting draught that came in under the canvas hood, and when she was safely out on the pavement once more she had looked down on the little car and smiled that bitter twisting smile with which he had grown so familiar, and had said, "Don't you think it's a little young for you, John". Then she had gone up the stairs to the house, a thin haggard woman, and had never mentioned the car again.

He had understood her; had understood her anguish, her need for drink, the books, the constant TV, but what he could not explain to her was that because of what had happened to their son and his family—terrible though it had been—*his* life was not over. How could he make her understand that he really did feel young enough to drive a sports car, young enough to accept the challenges that came to him every day, young enough to dominate a board meeting, young enough to want to impose his will on men still younger? How could he explain that to a woman who was simply a dry husk.

When they were first married it had been she who had driven him forward. That had been a few years after the war when he was still in a kind of limbo after what had happened to him in Berlin. He had never spoken of it, never, but she had sensed some deep emotional shock and had pulled him through that period. And then they had been married and his father had died and he had taken over the small engineering works in Battersea which he had expanded into the John Spencer Group of Companies, with three factories on the outskirts of London.

Now Margaret was dead and he was alive and married to Sue with a new family on the way and happier than he had ever been in his life. He had been given a second chance and he was making the most of it.

Susan had put his post on his desk and he began to go through it. There were a dozen or so brown envelopes that meant bills. As he looked through them he heard her begin to move in the room above him and after a few minutes she came down to the door of his study and said, "I'm going to make a salad and then I'll put the steaks on".

"Fine."

"Oh, I nearly forgot. Someone phoned two or three times while you were away. He had a foreign accent; sounded German."

"What did he want?"

"To check when you were coming back."

"German? It couldn't have been Dutch could it?"

"Could have been, I suppose. Anyway he phoned again today and I said you'd be home this evening."

She went to the kitchen on the ground floor and he could hear her begin to prepare the meal. He turned back to the mail. Rate bill, TV repair bill, water, electricity, all the old familiar horrors. At the bottom of the pile was a white envelope. On the front was written "Mr John Spencer", with a line under the name. That was all. No address. No postmark. No stamp. Which meant that it had been delivered by hand. Frowning he slit it open then shook it and something fell out onto the green leather top of his desk. It was a piece of black cloth about two inches square on which was embroidered in silver thread the heraldic device of three leopards superimposed on a bolt of lightning. There was no lettering. No other clue to what it was. It lay there innocent yet malevolent, harmless yet dangerous, inert yet powerful. He stared at it grimly. There wasn't one person in five million who would know what that small piece of cloth represented. But Spencer did.

\*        \*        \*

In Hyde Park too the drizzle had stopped and broken cloud had reached London. The moon was two-thirds full and its intermittent appearance gave the grass a silvery glow. Jurgen

13

Muller and Louis Tellier finished zipping themselves into their track-suits and climbed out of the Volkswagen.

"It is more cold," Tellier said, shivering.

"Never mind, it is dry."

"Which way?"

"He starts from down there at the other side." Muller pointed to the end of the Serpentine closest to Park Lane. "Then he comes up here, past the boats, over the bridge, and back past where there is swimming. Twice. Then back to the hotel."

"Which way do we go?"     .

"The other side."

They jogged through the car park, up and over the bridge, passing the restaurant on their left, then off the carriageway again and down towards the swimming area. As they approached the narrow end of the lake they slowed their pace until they came to a stop and began to do exercises. Away to their right a man was walking his dog, but after a few minutes he disappeared in the direction of Knightsbridge and they had the place to themselves.

"There he is," Muller said, and Tellier saw a single figure come running into the park. "Let him get to us."

Muller and Tellier began to jog again and soon they were leading the single runner by thirty or forty yards. He, too, was dressed in a dark track-suit and running shoes. He was a man of middle height with long curly hair that hung almost to his shoulders. From the rear he might have been mistaken for a woman but his face was thin and angular on top of a wiry body and as he ran one might have observed a steely springlike quality in his muscular rhythm, a sense of purpose. His name was Werner Riemeck. He had been born in the Berlin suburb of Spandau forty-one years before, and he had always tried to keep himself fit. Above all things he feared a stroke. Jogging was supposed to be good for the heart so whenever he could, he jogged.

He had only been in London for five days but it had not taken him long to discover that Hyde Park and the Serpentine were almost deserted by nine o'clock. The English, it seemed, were not so health-conscious as the Germans.

On this particular evening he noticed the two other joggers immediately he entered the park. He had grown used to having the place to himself and he resented the intrusion. He decided to pass them, then he would not have to look at them. He turned the corner at the east end of the Serpentine and began to run in the direction of the boathouse and the car park. The two joggers were thirty yards ahead and he increased his pace and began to draw up on them. Twenty yards ... fifteen ... ten ... The taller of the two men stopped and bent to tie the lace of his running shoe. The other man slowed down almost to walking pace. Riemeck put on a spurt; he could pass them now without embarrassment, without seeming to make a race of it.

"Good evening," he said in English as he ran between them.

The man in front of him, wearing the mountaineer's knitted hat turned away without answering. This surprised him, for the English were usually a well-mannered race. Perhaps he hadn't heard. There was a slight noise behind him; the scraping of a shoe on gravel. The man in the mountaineer's cap seemed to get in his way. Then a voice behind him said, *"Guten Abend, Werner"*.

Riemeck reacted without conscious thought. He flung his body to the left and felt hands grab his back, then slip off.

*"Schnell!"* the voice said.

The man in front had something in his hand, a length of wood or pipe.

Riemeck saw the water. He splashed into it. He tried to dive. Arms grabbed him around the waist. He felt a blow high up on his shoulder and burning pain down the length of his arm. He fought back, wrenching his body from side to side. He leant back, then jerked forward, bringing his captor off his feet. He twisted so that the man fell beneath him. The water was about two feet deep. He pressed down, holding the man under, trying to drown him. Then came the second blow. This one was more accurate.

\*       \*       \*

Spencer and his wife ate in the kitchen. "All right?" she said, meaning the steak.

"Perfect." He had tried to retain some of the mood of the early part of the evening, chatting about America, as if nothing had happened and all the time cold fingers were touching his stomach and bowels and finally, like a clock, he ran down and was silent.

"You're tired," she said.

"I shouldn't be, I've gained five or six hours flying this way. It's really only the middle of the afternoon by my time."

He helped her clear up and stack the dishes in the dishwasher. He'd offered her a maid when they were married but she'd said a "daily" would be enough and so Mrs Collins came in five days a week from nine till two. It had worked well because Sue was a good cook and liked to have the kitchen to herself, and it suited Spencer who had never liked servants under foot.

"I think I'll go up," Sue said. "The strain of having my husband back is beginning to tell." She put up her hand and touched his face. "Are you coming?"

"In a little while."

"Don't be too long. I'll get lonely." She went up to the bedroom and he heard her switch on the TV. He pictured her in bed propped up on the pillows and again fear touched him. He had wanted to ask her about the envelope but she might have questioned him. Would he have told her? The secret had been buried for so long he found it unthinkable he should share it. He had never been able to tell Margaret and he would never be able to tell Sue. Every fraction of her love and respect was of infinite value to him and he would do nothing to jeopardize it.

He went back to his study and sat down at his desk and stared out at London lying below. But between the room and the twinkling lights was the ghostly image of himself reflected in the window. He saw a man with a square face that was softening somewhat at the edges but still looked ten years younger than his real age. This was partly due to his hair which was as thick as it had ever been and still mostly dark except for the line of white above his left ear where once the skin had been opened to the bone. When the hair grew again it had come

16

up white and in an odd way it gave him a more interesting, more arresting appearance. Now the face looked older, grim. The cheeks were drawn, the jaw muscles knotted.

He opened the drawer and took out the piece of cloth with the three heraldic leopards. The moment he had opened the envelope earlier in the evening he had seen in his mind a series of vivid pictures of Bruno: Bruno at the house in Berlin; Bruno primping, showing off the uniform: "Look, Johnnie." and he had turned slowly like a mannequin, "Don't you like it?"

That was when Spencer had first seen the leopards. They had been sewn onto the collar of the field-grey jacket.

Astley had died in the bombing of Berlin. Richards had died fighting the Russians. There had been others, of course, but he had never met them. Just the three: Astley, Richards and Bruno. And if Astley was dead and Richards was dead, then Bruno had sent it. And that meant he was alive: that was ultimately what the piece of cloth meant. All these years he had hoped Bruno was dead. That had been part of the wall of confidence he had built around himself when he'd come out of that limbo after the war.

He tried to remember Bruno as he had first seen him, tall, blond, Aryan, good-looking, but wherever he placed him— walking down the Kurfurstendam, at the house in Charlottenburg, or the battered villa in Graf Speestrasse—the picture would deliquesce, only to reform as it did in all his nightmares. The dreams were reality, reality dreams. It was always the cellar with the body, always the animal, and always Bruno. What did he want now, Spencer wondered? How would it affect his life? That it would have an effect he had no doubt; Bruno never did things without purpose. Money? Was that it? And if he didn't pay? There was no statute of limitations as far as he knew. Prison? The ruination of his career? And what would happen to Sue? No, he'd pay all right. And Bruno knew that. How much, he wondered, did Bruno think his secret worth?

Just then the doorbell rang, cutting shrilly across his thoughts. He put the piece of material back into the envelope and dropped it into the top drawer of his desk. The bell went again. He could hear the TV on in the bedroom upstairs which meant that Sue would not have heard it. He looked at his watch. It was after nine. Who could it be at this time of night? Did it have something to do with Bruno? Could he ignore it? Pretend no one was home? The bell rang again, a shrill screaming in his ears. He ran quietly down the stairs into the sitting-room from the window of which he could see the front porch. A young woman was standing there.

He went into the hall, switched on the outside light and opened the door. She was in her late twenties and at her feet was a leather travelling bag. She was holding a newspaper in her hand.

"Good evening," he said. "Can I help you?"

"I have come for the room." She spoke a heavily-accented English.

"What room?"

"The room which you advertise."

"There must be some mistake. I haven't advertised a room."

"Here. It says in the local paper. Look." She held the *Hampstead and Highgate Express* towards him.

"I'm sorry, but I didn't place any advertisement."

"Is this . . ." And she mentioned the number of the house. ". . . Cannon Place, London north west three?"

"Yes, of course it is . . ."

"Look what it says!"

"I don't care what it says. I'm telling you . . ."

"Here."

Unwittingly, he bent to the paper. It was folded in four and as he did so she raised one of the folds and he found himself looking into the barrel of a pistol. "Continue, please, to look at the newspaper," she said. "Continue to look and you will not be hurt. Now ask me to come into the house."

He was staring at the gun.

"Ask!"

"Will you come in?"

"Thank you." He turned to go in first and she stopped him. "Where are your manners? You English are supposed to have

18

manners." He paused and let her pass him. Even in his confusion he realized that they were playing out a charade for any
watching neighbours. "Now close the door." He did as she
ordered. She threw down the paper and held the gun.

"Put out the light."

"Who are you?"

"Put out the light."

He switched off the outside light and the hall was plunged
into darkness.

She went to a narrow window by the side of the door and
looked out. "Keep back against the wall," she said. He heard
the sound of footsteps on the path. She opened the door, keeping well out of sight and Muller and Tellier, carrying a third
man between them as though he were drunk, came in the
door. In their free hands each carried a flight bag.

"What happened?" the woman asked.

"Tellier was too strong," Muller said.

"He was killing you," Tellier said.

"We have a problem with him." Droplets of water still clung
to Muller's beard.

"Take him in here," the woman said.

They went into the drawing-room on the left side of the hall.
"Wait." She crossed and closed the heavy velvet curtains. "All
right, put the light on." The men lowered Riemeck into one of
the big, chintz-covered armchairs and Spencer, standing in the
doorway, could see that he was unconscious, his head lolling to
one side. Muller said something to the woman in German and
Tellier turned swiftly. "Hey, in English only."

The girl shrugged. "All right." She looked at their sopping
clothing and said again, "What happened?"

"Riemeck tried to get away in the lake," Muller said.

"Maybe he could drown you," Tellier said viciously.

For the first time they seemed to notice Spencer standing
inside the drawing-room door.

"What do you want?" Spencer said.

Tellier went into the hall. "Is this the only telephone?"

"Yes."

"If you lie . . ."

"There are three extensions," Spencer said, trying to keep calm, to control his rage, "but this is the only outside line."

Tellier took a small pair of pliers from his flight bag and cut the wire.

Muller crossed the floor and stood in front of Spencer. "I have a message: Bruno sends his love."

Spencer stared at him.

"He sent you a little gift."

"I have it."

"How do you say it in English: a memory?"

The girl laughed, a short harsh sound. "A memento."

"*Ja*," Muller said. "A memento. Inge speaks good English. She was a teacher. She taught here in . . ."

"That's enough!" Inge said.

Spencer looked at her closely for the first time. She had a thin, sallow face and a thin body, with surprisingly heavy breasts. Her blonde hair was crimped and he guessed it might be a wig. She exuded a quality of dominant sexuality.

"Don't talk to me like that," Muller said.

"Stop bitching!" Tellier said.

"She's in heat," Muller said, smiling. "Don't worry, *liebchen*, I'll give it to you soon."

The girl looked at him in distaste. "You're crude," she said.

"Maybe I was not brought up like you," Muller said, suddenly angry. "Maybe my father was not a famous architect. I've still got something you want, though."

There was a groan from the chair. Muller stared down at Riemeck. "Werner!" he said. "Werner!" Riemeck's head did not move. Muller slapped him lightly on the cheek but he did not flinch. Muller turned to Tellier: "Only a gorilla would have hit so hard!"

Tellier had been standing at the window and now he turned. "There is someone in the house next door. The window facing this."

Muller moved to the curtain, then turned. "I don't like it here," he said to Inge. "What about the back?"

"I'll see." She went into the hall.

"You," Muller said to Spencer. "Come here."

Spencer took three steps towards him, then said again, "What are you going to do?"

"That is not your business. Your business is to be silent. All we want from you is your house. You keep your mouth shut and everything is all right."

Inge came in. "There is a room at the back on the next floor."

"Let's move him."

Muller and Tellier picked up Riemeck, carried him upstairs to Spencer's study and placed him on the buttoned leather Chesterfield. As they did so Spencer could see the angry red welt high up on his neck where a blow had landed.

"Get some water," Muller said to Tellier.

"Where?"

"I don't know where. Find some."

"There's a kitchen downstairs," Spencer said.

Muller went to the window, opened it, satisfied himself that the room was not overlooked, closed it and drew the curtains. Inge was looking at the stereo equipment and cameras. "Our newspapers tell us England is a poor country. But this . . ." She waved a hand at the gleaming array. "This is like the raspberry Reich."

Muller picked up one of the Nikons. "Japanese," he said. "German Leicas are better."

"Better not to have it at all," Inge said. "Better to learn consumption abstinence."

"Consumption abstinence!" Muller laughed. "Remember that lecture at the Free University? Consumption abstinence and praxis!" He spoke in German again. She nodded warningly in Spencer's direction but Muller said, "He probably can't understand and even if he could, what can he do?"

Spencer's German was rusty, but good enough to follow the exchanges. "Who *are* you?" he said.

Muller put down the camera and began to play with the stereo equipment. "You have heard of the R.A.F.?" At first the letters meant only one thing to Spencer, then his mind made the adjustment. "Something to do with a Red Army," he said.

"The Red Army Fraktion," Muller said. "We are Kommando Fritz Meinhardt."

"But what do you want with me?"

"I told you, we only want your house."

Tellier came in with a pot of water. Muller took it from him and poured it on the unconscious man's face. He groaned, but did not wake.

"He needs a doctor," Spencer said.

The four of them stared down in silence at Riemeck. Just then there were the clear sounds of footsteps from the room above. Guns appeared. Muller took a machine-pistol from his flight bag. "Who is that?" he said.

Spencer said, "My wife."

Muller turned to Inge. "You forgot the wife."

"You were late. I thought something had gone wrong. I'm sorry."

"I'm sorry," Muller mimicked her.

He turned to Spencer. "Fetch her."

"She's ill."

"Fetch her!"

"Look, there's nothing she can do. I've co-operated, haven't I?"

Muller pushed past him and made for the door. Spencer said "All right, I'll . . ."

"Wait here!" Muller pointed the gun at him. "I say things only once."

Spencer, Tellier and Inge heard his footsteps on the staircase, then a stifled scream. Spencer said, "For God's sake!" and made for the door. Tellier held his pistol to his chest. "You want this?"

A few moments later Muller appeared with Susan. Her face was ashen. Spencer pushed past Tellier and took her hand. "Has he hurt you?" She shook her head. He noticed that her lips were white.

"Ill!" Muller said, and laughed. "Ill from too much—" He made obscene motions with his right hand. He was holding the machine-pistol slackly in his left hand and Spencer saw a chance. Pretending to put his arm about Sue's shoulders he

22

struck down with the sharp side of his hand on Muller's forearm. The big man gave a grunt of pain as his arm became paralysed. The gun dangled for a moment, then fell. Spencer swooped on it, gathering it in his hands. He flung himself against the wall and turned so that he could cover them all. He stopped dead. Tellier had acted with as much speed as Spencer himself. He had grabbed Susan's arm, twisting it up under her shoulder blades. Her gasp of pain was softer than Muller's had been, but Spencer heard it just as well. He also saw Tellier's gun. It was pointed at the back of her head.

"Put it down," Tellier said. "With this—" He pronounced it "wiz zis", and it might have been comic at any other time. "—I can blow away her face."

Slowly, Spencer laid the machine-pistol on the floor. Muller stood rubbing his forearm, trying to bring back feeling in his fingers. Abruptly he let fly with his right hand, catching Spencer across the face with the back of it. "You wish it so," he said. Spencer took most of the blow on his nose. His eyes began to water and he could feel the blood drip down onto his lips and chin. Tellier pushed Susan towards him and she would have fallen had he not caught her.

"What do they want, John?" she said.

"I don't know." He took out his handkerchief and dabbed at his nose.

She sat down on his office chair. Riemeck groaned and stirred. He moved his legs and tried to sit up but the effort was too much for him and he fell back on the Chesterfield. Spencer noticed that a little blood was oozing from his right ear. *"Werner,"* Muller said, standing over him. *"Raus!"*

"There is no help shouting at him," Tellier said.

"You wake him, you hit him."

"He would have drowned you!"

"You think so. My foot slipped, that's all."

"Stop it!" Inge said.

"What are they saying, John?" Sue asked.

"It's about something that happened to him." He pointed to Riemeck.

"Is he badly hurt?"

"One of them hit him."

"But why bring him here?"

"I've no idea."

"Shut up," Muller said. "No talking."

"I only asked if he was badly hurt." There was anger in her voice and Spencer heard it with alarm. This was no situation for anger, it had to be played as cool as ice.

"It's not your business," Muller said.

"I took a nursing course once."

"A nurse?" Muller's tone was disbelieving.

"If he was hit on the head he's got concussion," she said.

"Brilliant. So what do we do?"

"You don't throw water on him."

"What then?"

"You need to keep him warm. There's an eiderdown upstairs and a hot water-bottle in the bathroom."

They wrapped Riemeck in the eiderdown and put a hot water-bottle at his back. His face was white and cold.

"How long will it take before he can talk?" Muller said.

"I don't know."

"I want a drink." He turned to Inge. "You too?"

She hesitated. "All right."

"I too," Tellier said.

"You get them. Where are they?" He turned to Spencer.

"In the drawing-room."

Tellier came back a few minutes later with three large whiskies. "That's better," Muller said, swallowing half his drink. "I'm hungry."

"Too much swimming," Tellier said.

"You are funny. Let her make something." He pointed at Susan.

Spencer shook his head grimly. "Leave my wife alone. I'll do it."

Muller opened his mouth to speak but Inge said, "Let her look after Werner. She's a nurse."

"You nurse him," Muller said to Sue. "If he wakes, you tell us, understand?" He cupped her chin in his hands. "*Verstehen Sie?*"

24

"Yes I understand."

They left her alone with Riemeck and when she was sure they had all gone downstairs she lifted the phone on Spencer's desk. The line was dead. She stood in the middle of the floor, uncertain and confused.

She was also very frightened. She had been dozing with the TV on when the big bearded man had come into the room. Her heart had almost stopped. He had told her to get up and numbly she had put on her dressing-gown and come down. With every step she took she became more and more frightened. And then she had seen John and the fear had lessened because John would cope. John always coped. She had known him first as an employer—she had been his secretary—and then as a lover and finally as a husband. At no time in any of the three roles had she ever doubted him. She had seen him cope with the affairs of his companies with a certain ruthlessness, but she had been in business herself for long enough to know that some ruthlessness was necessary. And she had been his mistress in the last year of Margaret's life and she had watched him cope with that problem. What had meant so much to her then was that he never lied to her. He was frank about Margaret's drinking and the cause of it and she knew, because he told her, that he would never leave Margaret. It was not an ideal arrangement for either of them but it was one she could arrange her life around. He never whined, he never promised more than he could make good. She knew exactly where she was at all times and when Margaret died and he asked her to marry him she never hesitated. The fact that he was more than twenty years older than she was hardly entered her mind.

Riemeck moaned again. She looked down at him. There was grey in his hair but with his eyes closed and his face deathly pale, he looked young and terribly vulnerable. What did they want with him? Was he one of them? If so why had they hurt him? Perhaps he wasn't one of them, perhaps he was an innocent member of the public like John and herself mixed up in something she did not understand? Or perhaps he was a hostage. Perhaps they were all hostages. If that were so then she must care for him as best she could. She had said she'd taken a nursing course; it was a St John's first aid course really and she could remember very little. She leant over Riemeck and touched his forehead. Some slight colour was coming back into his cheeks and he felt less clammy.

Suddenly his eyes opened and he stared up at her. *"Wer sind Sie? Wo bin ich."*

"I don't speak German," she said.

He reached back and felt the ridge of red flesh where he had been hit.

"Do you understand English?" she said.

"English?"

"I don't speak German. I'm English."

*"Ach, ja, Englisch."* He raised himself and sat for a moment, his head on his hands, then turned to her and said, "Where am I?"

"You're in a house in Hampstead in London."

"How did I get here? How did I get wet?" The one certain thing about concussion, she knew, was the inability to recall recent events.

"I don't know. I think you were brought."

"Who brought me?"

"Your friends."

"I have no friends here."

*"Ach, so, Werner."* The door had opened silently and Muller was there. "When did he wake?"

"Just now." She could feel a change in the man sitting next to her. He seemed to have tightened like a fist.

"I told you to tell me."

"It's only been a few seconds."

"What has he said?"

"He spoke German. I didn't understand."

"All right, out." He turned and called, "Inge! Tellier! Werner is with us."

The others joined him. They were both holding glasses.

Susan went down the stairs and joined her husband in the sitting-room. "The phone doesn't work," she said.

26

"I know. They cut it."

"Who are they?"

"Terrorists."

"Why us?"

"I don't know."

"What are we going to do?"

He walked over to the window, drew the curtain aside and looked out onto the quiet London street. The trees still bore their autumn leaves, the street lamps spread a cosy glow, the houses opposite, with their drawn curtains and chinks of light, looked safe and normal. He could even see the disc on the wall of an opposite house which marked the fact that the Egyptologist, Sir Flinders Petrie, had once lived there. It was so ordinary, so everyday.

He took her in his arms and held her as tight as he dared. "Listen," he said, "I don't know who these people are, and I don't know what they want. I don't *care* what they want. But they're armed and they're dangerous. They say they're a commando from the Red Army Fraktion." She looked mystified. "It's a German left-wing terrorist organization. I think it has links with terrorist groups in Japan and France. They don't play about. They've left a trail of killings all over Europe."

"Is that what they're here for?" She thought of the damp hair, the pale, vulnerable face. "Have they come to kill him?"

"God knows."

"Are we just going to let them?"

"Can you tell me how to stop them!"

"You've got a gun."

"Forget it. You saw what happened when I tried."

"But we can't just *let* them."

"Don't you understand: *They can do as they like.*"

"Here? In our house?"

"Of course."

"And we can't do anything?"

"Nothing."

"But they're not guarding us. We could run. Get help. Why aren't they guarding us? Why?"

He had been waiting for this. How could he tell her about Berlin now? About Bruno? About the leopards? Even if he had wanted to there was no time to make her understand. "Look at yourself," he said. "Do you think you could run for it? How far do you think you'd get?"

She seemed to accept that her unwieldiness might preclude that idea, but then she said, "But you could go, John."

"And leave you? What do you think they'd do to you?"

"Oh my God, John, there must be something!"

"It's not our business, Sue. They've come to do something. I don't know what. Out of all the houses in London, in Britain, they've chosen ours to do it in. There's no use asking me why, I don't know. I say let them kill each other, that makes one less terrorist in the world."

"He didn't look like a terrorist to me."

"What does a terrorist look like?"

"Not like him anyway. John, he was frightened and confused. He didn't know where he was or who we were or anything. And then the big bearded man came in and I could feel the terror. We can't allow . . ."

"Darling!" He gripped her by the shoulders, feeling the fragile bone structure under his fingers. "Listen to me! It's not a question of allowing or not allowing, we have no choice. We stay in here. We mind our own business. We keep our mouths shut. We do as they tell us. And then maybe . . . just maybe, we'll live."

At that moment there was a noise from the study. It was part scream, part moan, and it splintered the silence of the house as a stone splinters glass.

Susan put her hands to her ears. The scream came again. She bent over, began to rock from side to side. "Do something!" she shouted. "Don't let them go on? Do something!"

They stood looking at each other. Silence gathered in the house once more. Inge opened the sitting-room door. "We will eat now," she said to Spencer. She turned to Susan. "He is unconscious, see if you can bring him round again."

"No," she said. Her hands shifted to her cheeks.

"For Christ's sake . . .!" Spencer began.

"You have nothing to say!" Inge said. "Nothing! You do as *we* tell you. If you do not, you are finished. You understand? Bruno will finish you?" She turned towards Susan. "Give her a drink and get her upstairs."

"No," Susan said again.

"You want us to go?"

"Yes! Oh, yes!"

"Then do as I say and the sooner we go. You understand that?"

"Yes, I understand."

Sue went up to the study, terrified of what she might find there. The man was lying much as she had left him and at first she could see no difference other than the fact that the blanket had been pulled down and the hot water-bottle lay on the floor. Something oddly familiar was lying next to the hot water-bottle. It was the pop-up toaster from the kitchen. The lead snaked across the floor to a wall socket. Then she saw the man's left hand. The fingers were ridged with sulphurous yellow-and-black lines. Around the ridges the skin was red. His face was covered in a sheen of sweat.

"Oh, my God," she said. She coughed and kept herself from being sick. For a second the terror that lay on the periphery of her mind swept over her and she found herself shaking. She turned to the door, running blindly away from the mutilated man. A hand caught at the front of her dressing-gown and almost lifted her off her feet. She looked up into Muller's face.

"Where are you going?"

"I—" she began. "I—"

"Don't trouble yourself so much, he is a fascist." She fought his hands but he held her easily. "Where are you running?"

Within the wider context of her confusion there were other basic things she did not understand. What had happened to John? Why wasn't he coping? And who was Bruno? She understood nothing and it made her angry.

"This is *my* house," she managed at last. "You can't— can't—you—I'm going to get the police. You can't stop me!"

He smiled and stood elaborately to one side. "Please," he said.

She began to go down the stairs. Spencer stood at the bottom. "I'm going to the police, John."

"Let her go," Muller said. "If she wants it so much."

Spencer stopped her half way down. "Don't you see he's having fun with you. He wants you to try. He wants you to go to the front door. Then he'll bring you back. He'll humiliate you. Don't you understand?"

The courage born of fright which had brought her this far suddenly drained out of her like bath-water. Sue found herself trembling again. "Can I have a drink?" she said.

"So," Muller said. "We understand each other." He turned to Spencer. "Give her a drink and get her back." He flicked a thumb upstairs. "The longer it is, the more dangerous for you, not so?"

Spencer took her into the sitting-room and poured a whisky. She took it neat, feeling the warmth go down her throat and spread out through her nerves.

"Are we going to do whatever they say?" she said.

He looked at her for a moment before replying and then said, "Yes."

She felt steadier after the whisky. She went into the kitchen. The three terrorists were seated at the table eating scrambled eggs and bacon. She ignored them, went to the fridge, took out a pint bottle of milk, picked up a tea towel and returned upstairs. She was better prepared now but even so the ridged fingers and burnt nails gave off a smell that sickened her. She soaked the tea towel in the milk and wound it round the injured hand. Then she raised the arm and placed it on the Chesterfield. He had turned onto one side and she tried to push him over so that he lay on his back. He turned easily and she wondered if fear and loathing were giving her strength. Then she realized he was moving himself. As he did, he spoke to her again. His face was near her ear and he whispered, "They are going to kill me. You must help."

"I will help you." She could hear him breathing. "Your hand is . . ."

"My hand is nothing. That is a beginning. When they have finished with the hand they are going to kill me."

"Yes," she said, there did not seem any point in prevaricating.

"Listen . . ." He whispered a telephone number and she repeated it. "Phone that number."

"They've cut the phone."

"You must help me."

"Yes. Yes, I will."

"How goes he?" She nearly fainted. She turned and saw Tellier with his ridiculous mountaineer's beanie, standing in the doorway.

"What?"

"What are you doing with him?"

"He's in shock."

"He is not awake?"

"No. We have to keep him warm. The bottle's cold. Can you fill it?"

She picked up the hot water-bottle and handed it to him. "Not out of the tap. Boil the kettle. It needs to be hot."

He took the blue hot water-bottle from her reluctantly. "I do not believe in this."

"It worked before. We wrapped him up and kept him warm. And he came to. That's what you want, isn't it? You want him awake so you can go on torturing him."

"Do not worry. He is fascist." It was said mechanically, without any emotion, as though it were a word become threadbare with use.

"Well?"

He took the bottle and she heard him go downstairs.

"We have a few minutes," she whispered. "What do you want me to do?"

"You must help me."

"Yes. Yes. But how?"

"I must have a weapon. You have knife?"

"In the kitchen. They'd see me."

"Look quickly for something. Anything."

Her eyes swept the room. She took in the tape-recorder, the

radio, the TV, the cameras. How did you defend yourself with those? Riemeck's face was ashen as he watched. Then she remembered the gun.

"My husband has a pistol," she said. "I don't know where he keeps it. Here, probably, there's nowhere else."

He tried to get to his feet but giddiness swept over him. When he could speak he said, "The desk."

"Yes. But I think he keeps the drawers locked."

But the top drawers were not locked, and she realized he must have been working when he was interrupted. The three drawers on the left-hand side were also unlocked. Here there were a jumble of spectacles, fuses, an elastic bandage, a pile of cassettes, an old squash ball, more papers, letters, a diary, but no pistol.

"The bottom drawer's locked," she said. "My husband must have the key."

"Force it," he said.

"I don't know how."

Again he tried to get to his feet, again the dizziness swept over him. Then he said, "Take the middle drawer out."

She pulled the drawer out and put it on the desk. She could see into the bottom drawer. It contained what looked like the sort of shoe-bag one took to school as a child. She lifted it out. She was right. Sewn into one corner was a tag which said, "Richard Spencer, Form IV, Arundel House." But it did not contain shoes. There was something small and heavy. She opened the draw-string and pulled out first a brush of the kind used to clean babies' bottles, then a small bottle of oil, a rag, and finally the pistol itself. She handed it to Riemeck, who slid open the breech with professional ease. The gun was loaded.

At that moment they heard Tellier on the stairs.

"Tell him you think I'm dying," he whispered, and lay back on the Chesterfield, the gun in his right hand under the blanket.

She was terrified again. Things had moved too quickly. How would she convince Tellier? What if he found the gun? What would he do to her?

"Here is the hot water-bottle," Tellier said. He was holding a slice of bread in his other hand. "Is he awake yet?"

She cleared her throat. "I—I think he's dying."

"You don't die from a little burn."

"The blow on the head," she said.

Tellier stood in the centre of the room. "Listen to his breathing," she said. "It's very light."

Tellier moved forward. As he did so she realized she had left the drawer on top of the desk. She had been standing between it and Tellier. Now she moved to keep it out of sight. He gave her the bottle and she hugged it to her chest. It was hot and gave some comfort. Tellier leant over Riemeck to listen.

He couldn't hear any breathing at all. He moved his ear to Riemeck's chest to listen for his heart. He couldn't hear that either. He lifted his head to call Muller and felt something hard on his neck. Then he found himself looking into Riemeck's eyes. "Stay as you are, Louis," Riemeck said. "It's a gun. Look." He brought the pistol away, let Tellier see it, then forced the barrel into his ear. "Now help me up, Louis. But be careful."

"Take it easy, Werner. Take it easy."

"You take it easy. Give me your arm. Slowly . . . slowly! If I fall you get one in the brain."

They came up from the Chesterfield in slow motion, Tellier with his arm about Riemeck. As the blood left Riemeck's head he felt his knees begin to buckle. "Tighter," he said, screwing the gun into Tellier's ear. In a few moments he began to feel better and his vision cleared. "Now come round." He shifted so that he was behind the Frenchman. "When we get to the stairs we go down sideways. You in front of me. Me with my back to the wall. Understand?"

"Yes."

"Where's your car?"

"In the road."

"We go there. Then you drive where I tell you. Understand?"

"Yes."

Riemeck turned to Susan. "Can you open the front door?"

"I think so."

"Go quietly. Take off your shoes."

The three began to descend the stairs to the ground floor. Susan went first, followed by the two men, locked together. They could hear voices in the kitchen, which was at the back of the house. No one in the kitchen could see the staircase but once they reached the hall they would be visible for a matter of seconds if anyone was at the kitchen door. At the bottom of the stairs Riemeck stopped. Susan looked at him and he nodded. Noiselessly, she crossed the carpeted hall and carefully unlocked the front door. There was the faintest clicking of the lock and the door swung open. As he moved towards it Riemeck felt the cold autumn air on his legs.

It was this draught that disturbed Muller in the kitchen. His senses, so finely attuned to danger for so long a period, were instantly alerted by something, he did not know what. Then he isolated it. There was a movement of cold air where there should not have been.

"Louis?" he called.

The two men were in the centre of the hall. "Say nothing," Riemeck said. He twisted so that they were walking backwards, Tellier shielding him from the kitchen area.

"Louis!" This time it was much louder.

"Answer him," Riemeck whispered.

"*Oui.*"

Muller came to the door of the kitchen but the two men were out of his line of sight. He looked up towards the first floor and called, "Everything all right?"

Riemeck forced the gun deeper into Tellier's ear. "*Oui,*" Tellier said.

It was this final acknowledgment which undid them. It came from the wrong part of the house. Muller reached for the machine pistol on the kitchen table and ran into the passage. The two men were almost at the door when he saw them.

"Jurgen!" Tellier began, but did not finish the sentence, or at least no one heard it, for Muller did not hesitate. He fired at the group, hitting Susan, then Tellier several times in the chest

34

before he fell to one side. Riemeck did not have time to aim his pistol. The bullets passed through Tellier and into him and soon he could no longer hold Tellier and his own body became the target.

Spencer ran from the kitchen, the sound of Susan's abrupt, cut-off scream in his ears. The bodies lay just inside the door. Smoke floated in layers on the still autumn air. Across the road curtains were being pulled back, lights were springing on. But inside the house everything was frozen, all movement stopped. The bodies lay upon each other in a tangled mass. He was barely aware of Muller and the girl pulling Tellier free and carrying him down the path to the street. He stood there, other visions bursting before his eyes, other arms and legs, other heads. The woman was no longer Susan, she was the woman in the cellar, the fingers dissolved even as he looked at them and became blue stumps, and above the body in the shadows . . . what? Was it there? Grey black . . . wolf-sable . . . ready to spring; to feed? He was aware of a great ringing cry; it filled the hall and poured out into the night. It took him some seconds to realize that the cry was coming from himself.

It was the cry that brought help; it was the cry that the neighbours mentioned; that the police heard of. They said it was the cry of a man whose loved one was killed before his eyes. But it was more than that; it was a cry that Dr Faustus might have made; it was a cry that sounded across an abyss where nightmares lurked, where Nemesis waited; it was a cry of recognition.

# London

## PART II

In the month that followed the murder of his wife and unborn child Spencer lived in a grim world of memories, remorse and rage, broken intermittently by visits from the police to his house and his own visits to Scotland Yard. He was questioned by members of the Terrorist and Bomb Squad and by Detective Chief Superintendent Nichols of E for Echo District, his local division. Later, permission was given for representatives of the German "Popos", the political police, and the "Kripos", the criminal police, to talk to him. He described what had happened, but made no mention of Bruno or of the heraldic leopards.

There were several press conferences set up by the police but he did not attend them. At first his house was besieged by press and TV reporters but he kept his mouth grimly shut and after a while they left him in peace. At the end of four weeks there was no question left to answer that had not been asked; nothing left to read in the police files that had not been read; no photograph left to see that had not been seen.

In these weeks immediately after the shooting it was Detective Chief Superintendent Nichols who kept him abreast of the investigation. And one evening he telephoned to say that the Volkswagen microbus had been found in a car park in Cosham in Hampshire. There was no sign of Tellier's body and it was assumed that the man and woman who survived had got rid of it in some forest or lake, or had buried it in the Queen Elizabeth Park. A search was carried out, but nothing was found.

Everything was an assumption. It was assumed that after they had got rid of Tellier's body the man and woman had walked into Portsmouth and caught the ferry for France. Another assumption was that the woman was no longer a blonde, the man no longer bearded. No one knew what they really looked like. In the rear of the VW the police had discovered a blonde wig made in Italy and two track-suits made in Korea. They had lifted a mass of fingerprints, but the few clear enough for identification had proved untraceable.

After Scotland Yard's forensic experts had gone over the Volkswagen it was taken to Hampshire police headquarters in Winchester and there two experts from the Berlin *Kriminalpolizei* were allowed to examine it. They set about taking the interior to pieces. For two days they found no more than their British counterparts, and then they had a stroke of luck. In forcing a panel out of the wardrobe one of the joints broke and they found, caught in the back of the panel, a small square of cloth with the heraldic device of three leopards on it. The German forensic experts did not share this piece of information with their British colleagues, and when they returned to Berlin they took it with them for identification.

At the end of four weeks the police left Spencer alone and even the telephone calls from Nichols became less frequent; there was nothing to report. For Spencer, the four weeks went by like four years. He was waiting, and time hangs heavy when you wait. He had tried to live a life as close as he could to the one he had lived before. He had gone to work and worked hard all day, but it was the evenings he dreaded. They lay in wait for him as autumn turned to winter. Some nights he went out and wandered through Soho and the West End because he could not face the empty house. On others he brought piles of work home and sat at his desk until two or three in the morning, filling the hours with work or TV or radio, anything that would occupy time in such a way as to blanket his thoughts.

But nothing was effective and he went over and over in his mind the events of that last evening, trying to see where it might have turned on a different path. If only Sue had done the cooking, if only she had not said she had taken a course in first aid, if he had been quicker when he had grabbed the gun, if . . . if he had never met Bruno . . .

His thoughts led him farther and farther back, for the springs of the shooting in Hampstead were locked in other

38

events more than a quarter of a century old. For most of his adult life he had tried to forget what had happened in Germany, but now his life had turned a corner and there they all were, waiting for him, the memories he had so carefully buried . . .

*    *    *

The first thing John Spencer could remember about his father, Wilfred Spencer, was the black shirt in which he would dress most Saturdays, and in which he would return either late on Saturday night or on Sunday morning, sometimes with bruising on his face and the skin off his knuckles. He was a small man with a toothbrush moustache and hair slicked down with brilliantine. When Spencer was older he had equated his father's militant fascism with his diminutive size. He was barely five feet four inches tall and in his own house he was something of a dictator. Spencer's mother, a colourless, introspective woman, was no match for him and he dominated the household like some tyrannical pygmy.

During the week John hardly saw his father, for he owned a small engineering works in Battersea which turned out the metal struts for shelving systems. The middle thirties was a bad time for small factory owners: markets were getting harder to penetrate, cheap goods were flooding in from Japan. This, Spencer was later to think, had been an added factor to cause his father to join the British Union of Fascists and adopt the black shirt as his uniform. In their sitting-room had hung portraits of Adolf Hitler and Benito Mussolini and opposite them, hanging above the mantelpiece, was a pokerwork slogan: "If you love your country you are a National. If you love her people you are a Socialist. Be a National Socialist." Underneath that was the name William Joyce. His father had known Joyce, who was later to leave Britain for Germany and become the propaganda broadcaster Lord Haw-Haw, and later still to be hanged by the British after the war for treason. He had come down to the house on one of his fund raising drives, for Spencer's father was the local treasurer. Spencer remembered vaguely a short square figure dressed in a muffler and trench coat and carrying a heavy blackthorn stick. One side of his mouth was twisted by a scar. But he had been friendly and had shaken Spencer's hand and talked to him about football.

The second time he had seen Joyce was at a meeting to which his father had taken him. It was on a Saturday afternoon and he could not have been more than seven or eight but he remembered the events of that day clearly. They had gone up to London in a charabanc hired by the South-East London Branch of the British Union of Fascists. The meeting was being held in the Albert Hall and the streets around it were already seething with demonstrators when they arrived. He remembered the rows of police in their dark blue uniforms, some holding truncheons, some dogs on leashes, some on horseback. In Kensington Gore and around the Albert Memorial groups were waving banners and surging up and down the pavements shouting "Red Front! Red Front! Red Front! United Front! Down with the Fascists!" and then singing the Internationale.

The charabanc had stopped at the back of the hall and some of the opposition groups had pelted it with tomatoes and eggs and had tried to smash the windows with the poles of their banners.

"Hold my hand," Wilfred Spencer had said to his son, "and don't let go of it, understand?"

John was frightened by the noise and the shouting and the antagonism and they had to sit in the charabanc for fifteen or twenty minutes until the police encircled it and made two lines to the rear door of the hall through which they could walk in safety.

Stewards checked their tickets and as they went into the hall he saw a group of young women being hustled out of the far door. "Zionists," his father had said. He recalled the heat in the hall and the crush. His father was later to tell him that the principal speakers had been Mosley and Joyce but he could not remember them or what they had said.

After it was all over a policeman took him back to the charabanc while his father paraded with the other Blackshirts up and down Kensington Gore defying the opposition groups.

40

Scuffles broke out, stones were thrown and when his father came back to the charabanc Spencer noticed that he had a cut on his right cheek which was bleeding. He looked stimulated, his eyes shone, and he seemed very pleased.

"One day we'll rule the country," he said. "Then we'll make them pay."

But when war broke out in 1939 hundreds of Blackshirts, many of whom had joined the organization just to wear the uniform or to brawl in the street or march or be gripped by the mass hysteria of the meetings, joined the army instead and put on other uniforms and went on other marches and fought a different opposition. Not Wilfred Spencer. He had really believed in Mosley and National Socialism and had seen Hitler and Mussolini as the great white hopes.

Soon after war was declared he bought himself a dachshund on the grounds that he wished to advertise where his sympathies lay. During World War I dachshunds had been stoned in British streets. But no one in Bromley paid much attention to the short fierce-looking man and the strangely-shaped dog as they went for their daily constitutionals. He sold his Morris car and bought a second-hand D.K.W., the German people's car. He kept the portraits of Hitler and Mussolini on the walls of the sitting-room, and in the evenings, Spencer recalled, his father would always tune-in, as thousands of others did, to Lord Haw-Haw's propaganda broadcasts from Berlin. Whereas most listeners did so to laugh and jeer, Wilfred Spencer sat crouched by the radio, drinking in every word. One of John's most vivid memories of the early part of the war was his mother tip-toeing about the sitting-room while his father twiddled with the knobs of the old HMV radio until he picked up the voice saying, "Chairmany calling. Chairmany calling".

Wilfred Spencer was twice investigated by the Special Branch. Once they came to the house at seven o'clock in the morning and went through his papers and the books on the bookshelves but the most damming evidence they could discover was a translation of *Mein Kampf* and there were thousands of those in the country.

Spencer's father paraded his feelings so remorselessly that

people eventually took notice. Little things began to happen. Their milkman, who had lost an eye at Dunkirk, finally refused to deliver their milk and when Mrs Spencer telephoned the dairy she was told briefly to find some other supplier. Then the local policeman on the beat, a man who had fought in World War I, took to standing outside their house for five and ten minutes at a time. Often he would stare in at the bow-windows. This attracted attention and once or twice after the pubs closed in the evenings a group of soldiers home on leave had pitched stones through the glass. Wilfred Spencer had gone down to the police station on both occasions but nothing had been done.

Spencer himself was at the local grammar school and it was here that he felt most severely the results of his father's attitude. They gave him the nickname Adolf and bullied him continuously. There were two places he feared most. One was the lavatory block where a group of boys older than he had held his head in the lavatory pan while one had pulled the chain. The other was an area of waste ground where a bomb had fallen in 1941 and which was now, two years later, still a mass of rubble and weeds. It was on his way home from school and twice he had been pulled behind one of the broken walls of what had been a large house, and beaten up. After that he went an extra half mile to avoid the place.

In 1944 when he was sixteen, Spencer had turned into a good-looking youth, almost girlish in complexion. And a new hazard arose. He found himself frequently being solicited by soldiers and sailors.

The fights at school were continuing and Spencer was consistently losing them. He had had rheumatic fever when he was fifteen and had still not recovered his strength. Things came to a head early in 1944. One evening his father was listening to the radio in the sitting-room, his mother was in the kitchen, and Spencer was upstairs in his bedroom reading Sabatini instead of doing his homework, when he heard shouting in the road outside. They lived in a detached house built in the late twenties; part of a street of houses of exactly the same design. His room was at the front and he looked from the window and saw three or four shadowy figures. There were no lights on because of the black-out and he could not make out who they were. Then there was a crash from downstairs. He heard his father swear. He ran downstairs and saw that a brick had been thrown through the sitting-room window. It had smashed the glass and brought down part of the black-out blind.

Just at that moment, through the hole formed by the brick, someone threw a brown paper parcel filled with human faeces. It hit the wall of the room and spattered over the sofa. Then the voice of the local air-raid warden shouted, "Put out that bloody light!" and there was a noise of running feet as the gang fled up the street. The following day Spencer tried to join the army.

He did not go to the local recruiting station in case he was recognized but instead he left school at lunchtime, changed his blazer for a tweed jacket and caught a bus to Lewisham. The recruiting sergeant was sitting behind a desk covered in forms. When Spencer told him he wanted to join the infantry the sergeant looked up and said, "How old are you son?"

"Eighteen."

"And you want to fight the Germans, do you?"

"Yes."

"Does your Mum know you've come?"

"Yes."

"And your Dad?"

"Yes."

"Are you on the telephone at home?"

"Y—No."

The sergeant was a grey-haired, fatherly-looking man who had been playing noughts and crosses with himself on one of the forms while he questioned Spencer. Now he put down the pencil and said, "Listen, son, I've seen hundreds come in here, some of them fifty years old and some of them your age. If you'd come in just after Dunkirk we might have taken you but we don't need you just now. We can wait until you've grown up a bit. So you hop it back home and no one'll know the difference."

But he did not go home. He used what little money he had to go on into London as far as the East India docks where he was taken on as mess boy in a freighter that sailed two days later for Liverpool. No one gave a damn about his age or whether his Mum had given him permission.

Spencer had never formulated any idea of what war was really like. He had read several novels about World War I and had seen the soldiers and sailors in the streets of south-east London with their girlfriends clinging to their arms. Like many of his generation he had identified with the uniform and what it brought. Reality was different. In the first place he was not fighting the Germans, in the second he had no uniform and in the third no formal or even discernible place in the scheme of things. He was the lowest form of life aboard and every unpleasant job from cleaning the lavatories to washing the saucepans in lukewarm greasy water, fell to him. On top of that he was seasick.

They joined a convoy assembling in Liverpool and sailed a week later for Russia. During that time the only thing he could recall doing was writing a letter to his mother telling her that he was at sea and that she was not to worry.

The *S.S. Coral Strand* had been built in the twenties for the jute trade and now, packed with spare parts for aircraft and tanks, she was like a derelict warehouse that had been pushed into the water. Rust streaked her deck housing and her engines were so worn and tired that she could barely manage eight knots. She was the slowest vessel in the convoy. Two hundred miles north-west of the Faroes she broke down completely. Spencer never knew what the trouble was, something to do with a bearing he was told, but for almost a day the ship was hove-to as her engineers tried to repair the damage. A destroyer was detached from the convoy escort to look after them. After nearly twenty-four hours they were still floundering in the heavy seas and the destroyer was needed on her station. They watched her go with despair. Six hours later they were torpedoed.

Up to that moment Spencer had been on the periphery of the war. He had got over his seasickness, but it had been replaced by constant exhaustion and any spare time he had he had crawled into his damp bunk and slept like the dead. Now he moved into the centre of the war where ships were blown out of the water and men were killed and lungs filled up with oil. Half an hour after the *S.S. Coral Strand* went down by the stern, he was picked up by a U-boat. He had swallowed a mixture of sea water and oil and for the next forty-eight hours he was in a semi-coma brought on by continuous vomiting. The medical orderly told the captain that he would never survive. But he did survive: the spasms grew fewer, the periods of quiescence longer and on the third day he began to get better. It was then he was told by the orderly, in a mixture of broken English and German, that he was his ship's only survivor.

A few days later he was transferred to the German oiler *Heide* where he was kept under hatches for nearly two months. He was the only prisoner aboard and the captain treated him with exaggerated caution in what amounted to solitary confinement. He took his meals alone, spent most of the day alone and was given half an hour's exercise on deck each afternoon.

The only contact he had with other human beings was the mess-hand who brought him his food. He was a young North German boy not much older than Spencer himself. At the beginning he was reserved and carried out his duties punctiliously, but after a week or so some of his reserve broke down. He brought Spencer a jig-saw puzzle and later Buchan's *Four Adventures of Richard Hannay*, an omnibus volume that had been left aboard by someone in the days of peace. The German could speak no English and Spencer no German but by pointing to dishes and cutlery and food, he quickly learned the German words applicable to meal times and the mess-boy learned what they were called in English. They began to teach each other their languages, and by the time the *Heide* berthed in Bremerhaven in the late spring of 1944 Spencer had a reasonable grounding in German.

The camp to which he was sent was situated a few miles outside Bremerhaven on flat, sandy soil surrounded by dark pine woods. It was a stark, functional-looking place. The compound was about two hundred and fifty yards square inside a double fence ten feet high. The space between the fences had been filled with coils of rusty barbed wire. About thirty feet inside the main fence ran the warning wire and inside this were the living quarters. They comprised twelve bare wooden huts in three rows. Beyond them was an area of hard-packed soil used for games and the twice-daily head count that was known to British and German alike as *appell*. Just outside the warning-wire was the *vorlager* containing the sick quarters, the punishment cells known to everyone as the "cooler" and the *kommandatur*, the administrative offices. Every hundred yards along the double fence was a sentry box and more sentries patrolled the fence on foot. As an additional precaution there were several *hundfuehrers* who patrolled with specially trained, savage-looking Alsatian dogs. The huts were divided into rooms about twenty feet square, each to be bedroom, dining-room and living-room for eight people. Furniture was sparse; double-decker bunks, a table, stools, lockers and a wood stove on a tiled base which stood in the corner. Each hut had a washroom, lavatory and a kitchen with a coal stove which had two burners and a small oven. Most of the cooking was done on the small stove though there was a cook house where they could get boiling water and sometimes cabbage soup. Spencer was sent to Hut Seven.

It took him some time to get his bearings in the camp. He never knew exactly how many men there were, somewhere between five and eight hundred probably. There were a dozen different nationalities: English, Scottish, Irish, Welsh, Indian, Goanese, Australian, Canadian; there were Lascars and even a Krooman from West Africa; they came from every part of the world where British Empire merchantmen recruited their crews.

At first he was pleased to be out of the solitary cell he had inhabited in the *Heide*, for in the camp, by comparison, discipline was lax, and provided he was on *appell* morning and afternoon and did not hang about the fences, he could spend his time very much as he liked. But it had its dangers, especially for a boy like Spencer. Most of the prisoners were stokers, deckhands and ordinary seamen; it was not an ideal place for a sixteen-year-old. Nor was he lucky with his fellow prisoners.

He was put in with some of the survivors of a Scottish freighter torpedoed nearly six months earlier. Her home port had been Leith and most of the men came from Edinburgh. They were a tough, clannish bunch who spoke a language of their own, hardly comprehensible to Spencer. They lived in a world of memory bounded by the pubs and whores of Rose Street on a Saturday night and the football fortunes of Hibs and Hearts. It was the wrong place for an Englishman to be and they didn't hide their prejudices. Most of the time they treated him with indifference. He was fitted into the roster of cooking and washing-up but apart from that he was ignored. He was not included in their discussions or their endless games of cards, nor did he share their Red Cross food parcels. He was pleased to be excluded, he found them physically dirty and was repelled by their eating habits. He could ignore them too, all except Campbell.

Campbell was a stoker about thirty years old, a big, bony man with broad calloused hands and a face covered by the healed scars of acne. From the beginning Spencer had been aware of Campbell. He was older than the other Scots and often did not join them at cards or reminiscing but would lie on his bunk reading "Superman" and "Green Lantern" comics, his lips forming the words as his eyes moved slowly across the page. And sometimes Spencer would look up from his own book and see Campbell's eyes on him.

One afternoon the others had gone out to play football against another hut and Spencer had fallen asleep in his upper bunk. He woke to feel a hand on his leg. His eyes opened and he looked directly into Campbell's face on a level with his own.

"What do you want?" he said jerking his leg away.

"I want tae ask a wee favour."

"What is it?" Spencer got down from the bunk and kept the table between them.

"I want you tae do something for me."

"What?"

"I'd no' ask if it wasnae important. But you're tae promise tae say nothing."

"That depends."

"Promise!"

At that moment Campbell looked unbalanced and Spencer began to move towards the door.

"Promise!"

"All right, I promise. What is it?"

"I want you tae write a letter for me."

It turned out that Campbell was illiterate and had been too shy to ask any of his fellow-Scots. Greatly relieved, Spencer wrote a letter on his behalf to his mother in Peebles. It was the first of several and it earned him Campbell's gratitude. He was not sure whether this was better than his indifference, for now when he found Campbell's eyes upon him, the big man would smile and he would be forced to return it.

There were other calls on his attention. One day, about six weeks after his arrival, *appell* was held an hour earlier in the afternoon. This was unusual and the men went to their positions speculating on the reason: some said the war was over, some that they were being moved to another camp, others that there was going to be an exchange of prisoners and that they were going back to Britain. But when they reached the recreation area they found that a small platform had been set up and a microphone had been connected to the loud-speaker system. *Appell* was taken, and then the *Kommandant* arrived, followed by another figure: short, square, and dressed in an old, trench-coat style macintosh. In his right hand he carried a walking stick. There was something familiar about him, then Spencer realized he was looking at William Joyce, whom he had last seen in his father's house in Bromley.

"We have here today an important British person," the *Kommandant* began by way of introduction. "Herr Joyce, who works in Berlin at the *Rundfunk* and broadcasts all over the world in the cause of the Fatherland and of peace. Herr Joyce wishes to say something to you today."

He gave a stiff bow in Joyce's direction and moved away from the microphone. It had been the briefest possible intro-duction and the *Kommandant* had looked uneasy. When the name Joyce was mentioned there had been a stir along the

48

lines of men, many of whom, like Spencer, had heard his broadcasts in Britain. Now, as he stepped to the microphone there were several shouts of "Traitor! Traitor!" and an undercurrent of booing. Joyce stood behind the microphone, staring down at the prisoners, the scar at the right side of his mouth giving an arrogant cast to his face. He waited for the jeering and booing to die down, then he said, "Men, we are fighting with the best of Europe's youth to preserve our European civilization and our common cultural heritage from the menace of Jewish Communism. Make no mistake about it: Europe includes England.

"Should Soviet Russia ever overcome Germany and the other European countries fighting with her, nothing on this earth would save the Continent from Communism and our own country would inevitably sooner or later succumb. We are British. We love England and all it stands for. Many of us have lost comrades, sacrificed in this war of Jewish revenge.

"We have always felt we were being lied to and betrayed. Now we know it for certain. This conflict between England and Germany is racial suicide. We must unite and take up arms against the common enemy!

"I ask you to come into our ranks and fight shoulder to shoulder with us for Europe and for England.

"Many of the other countries of Europe: Norway, Holland, Sweden, even Spain have sent their sons to fight with us. Now we are asking you to join such a force, but made up of Britons. It is called the British Free Corps, and is being formed in Berlin.

"Anyone who wishes to join will be taken from this camp to special training facilities in Berlin where there is good food, good wine and not so good women."

There was an ironic cheer at this. Spencer had noticed that at first the magnetism of his personality and his voice had grabbed the unwilling attention of the audience, but this ironic cheer broke the spell. Men began to talk to each other and shuffle their feet. Joyce went on at some length about this new fighting unit. He described how hundreds had joined from other prisoner-of-war camps. He spoke of the dedication

49

needed, of the pay, and how they would be making themselves useful instead of decaying behind barbed wire. But, above all, he repeated the need for a united stand to conquer Jewish Communism.

At the end of the speech the men were dismissed and Spencer walked back, feeling uneasy and ashamed that he knew Joyce. As they went back to their huts each man was given a pamphlet about the British Free Corps. Some dropped them in the dirt, others stuffed them in their pockets to be used later as lavatory paper.

The weeks went by. Summer gave way to autumn. Allied troops were fighting on the Continent of Europe and it was said that the war was going to end any day. It did not. It lingered on. But everyone, including the German guards and administrative staff, now knew that it was only a matter of time before Germany was over-run. Discipline became lax, punishments less severe; no one wished to be remembered as being a tyrant once the war was over. It was in this atmosphere that Spencer's relationship with Campbell reached crisis point.

The big stoker had been forcing his company more and more on Spencer, so that he had taken to playing cricket and football to get away from him. Then, one day in October, the Scots crew got hold of liquor.

For some weeks they had been talking about ways and means, and then there was a surge of Red Cross parcels and they pooled their chocolate and bribed one of the guards. Spencer was not sure what the drink was because it came in unlabelled bottles. It had a pungent smell which reminded him of kerosene, but the men didn't seem to mind. They drank it in enamel mugs, coughing each time they took a mouthful.

"Ma Gawd," one of them said, "this'll put something in yer trews."

They drank and talked and played cards and Spencer lay on his bunk trying to read. After a while one of them said, "Gie us a tune, Archie".

"Aye, come on then."

Archie took out a concertina and began to play, "I Belong

to Glasgow", and they sang that, and "Loch Lomond", and "Cock o' the North", and then Campbell, got to his feet and said, "Come on, lads, an eightsome. Gie us a reel, Archie."

The music grew louder and the men began to dance a mixture of an eightsome reel and the "Dashing White Sergeant". A chair was knocked over and broken and two of them crashed into a tier of bunks.

"Steady, lads, or we'll be in trouble," Archie said. He began to play a waltz. Several of the men began to dance, some taking the women's parts.

"How about a turn, ma wee lassie." Spencer looked up startled.

Campbell was standing by the bunk. His big face was red and sweaty. Spencer noticed his hands again, huge and square: coal dust was ingrained at the sides of his nose.

"I don't feel like it," he said.

"I'm no askin', laddie, I'm tellin'."

He pulled Spencer out of the bunk and they began to dance. At first it was not more than drunken fun. They danced waltzes and foxtrots, and other seamen cut in from time to time. Then one or two of them staggered off to their bunks and Archie was sick over his concertina, the lights flickered once, then went off, and Spencer was left with Campbell. Suddenly everything changed. They were in a corner of the hut that could not be seen from the sleeping area when he felt Campbell's hands on his trousers trying to unbutton his flies.

"Take your hands off me!" he said.

"Och, we're only having a bit o' fun."

He tried to pull away but the stoker's arms were like iron. He put his face next to Spencer's and he smelled the reek of liquor. "You're a pretty wee thing," Campbell said.

"Let me go!"

"I've nae had a woman for a year."

Spencer fought silently and ineffectively. He could feel his trousers being pulled down. "Wha's a bit o' fun?" Campbell said. "We're aw entitled to a wee bit o' fun."

The stoker's hands were between his legs and he shouted at

51

the top of his lungs, but no one in the hut stirred. He felt the power of the big man and knew that in a moment he must fall. Campbell was so drunk he could barely keep his balance and it was this that helped Spencer. He had been pushing Campbell and the big man seemed to lose his balance and his shoulder went through one of the hut windows. There was a splintering of glass followed almost immediately by shouts and lights and the hut was swarming with guards. Campbell and Spencer were grabbed. Campbell fought and was finally silenced with a rifle butt. Then they were dragged to the cooler and placed in adjoining cells.

Campbell was awake the following morning when the *Kommandant* sent for Spencer. He was standing at the door of his cell gripping the bars with his huge hands. There was an expression of anger on his dark face. "You listen tae me, lad: one word—one bloody word—and I'll finish you."

The camp *Kommandant* was a pragmatist, The last thing he wanted at this stage of the war was trouble.

"I've been waiting for something like this," he said, looking first at Spencer and then at his file. He stood up, a loose-jointed man with a high-domed bald head, and walked to the window which looked out onto a bleak prospect of barbed wire and sentry boxes. "Sixteen years old! I told them at the beginning what would happen. They said there was nowhere else to send you. You should be at home with your father and mother, Spencer, not here giving me trouble." He came back, slumped in his chair "What to do with you, that is the question, eh? You are a problem to me. Wherever I put you the same thing is going to happen. Oh, don't bother to lie to me, I can guess what happened. A man of thirty years and nearly one hundred kilos fighting with sixteen years. Don't you think I know? You cannot have a command like mine and live like a saint. There are no saints here, Spencer, that is why I worry about you. Did he threaten you?"

"Yes, sir."

"If you spoke about it?" He moved back to the desk.

"Yes, sir."

"He will try again one day and if you don't give him what

he wants he will hurt you badly; maybe even kill you. It is not nice to think about."

Spencer agreed. During the night in the cooler when he had been unable to sleep he had felt sick with apprehension at the thought of the future. He knew that Campbell would have another go at him and he knew that Campbell's mates would do nothing to stop him.

"Sir," he said. "Couldn't you transfer me to another camp?"

"At this time in the war it is not possible. There are no arrangements left for such things."

"To another hut, sir."

"Don't you understand that what happened to you with Campbell can happen in any hut! You are a problem, Spencer. You are too good-looking. Has such a thing never happened before?"

He remembered the soldiers and sailors in the streets of south-east London. But theirs had been friendly advances compared to Campbell's.

"I cannot leave you with Campbell, that is certain," the *Kommandant* said. He began moving papers about on his desk, putting one on top of the other, shuffling them, rearranging them. At last he pulled one up and studied it. He looked thoughtfully at Spencer for a moment, then said, "Perhaps you will have more chance against the Russians than against Campbell. Have you read this?" It was the pamphlet that had been distributed to the men after William Joyce's speech.

"No."

"Go into the office next door and read it. Think very carefully. Take your time. Understand it. Understand what you are doing and how it will affect you when the war is over. Then come and tell me your decision."

He went into an empty room next to the *Kommandant's* office and looked at the piece of paper. It was headed "British Free Corps". He began to read:

"As a result of repeated applications from British subjects from all over the world wishing to take part in the common

53

European struggle against Bolshevism, authorization has recently been given for the creation of a British Volunteer unit. The British Free Corps publishes herewith the following short statement of the aims and principles of the unit:

1. The British Free Corps is a thoroughly British volunteer unit conceived and created by British subjects from all parts of the Empire who have taken up arms and pledged their lives in the common European struggle against Soviet Russia.

2. The British Free Corps condemns the war with Germany and the sacrifice of British blood in the interests of Jewry and International Finance, and regards this conflict as a fundamental betrayal of the British people and British Imperial interests.

3. The British Free Corps desires the establishment of peace in Europe, the development of close friendly relations between England and Germany, and the encouragement of mutual understanding and collaboration between the two great Germanic peoples.

4. The British Free Corps will neither make war against Britain or the British Crown, nor support any action or policy detrimental to the interests of the British.

Published by the British Free Corps."

He read the leaflet three times. He had always despised the fascists as symbolized by his father, but he saw no conflict now in accepting the way out that the *Kommandant* was offering. His experience of those who were fighting fascism had been little better. He went back to the *Kommandant*.

"Do you understand it? Will you go?"

"Yes, sir."

"All right." He paused for a moment and then looked up. "I will put on your papers that you were sent to Berlin because you were too young for the camp. It might help after the war when you are interrogated. Do you understand?"

"Yes, sir. Thank you, sir."

. . . . .

Spencer stood at the window of his study in the house in Hampstead and stared down on the lights of London. It was a cold and frosty night and they were particularly brilliant. It was six weeks since the terrorists had been in the house, since Sue, Tellier and Werner Riemeck had been killed, and still the investigation seemed to have got nowhere, except that the police now knew that the Volkswagen had been stolen from a parking lot in Stuttgart; it had been owned by an American couple on a touring holiday. Apart from that, there was nothing, or at least nothing that the police were confiding to Spencer.

When he looked back over the six weeks, the hours and days seemed to blur. There had been so many questions and so many policemen asking them that he could no longer differentiate one question from another, one policeman from the next. The daylight hours, which he spent at his office, could also not be differentiated. He was picked up by his driver in the Mercedes at eight and returned at seven, day in, day out, including Saturdays. There had been an attempt on the part of one or two senior executives in the company to take the work load off his shoulders, and a suggestion that he go away for a month or two and forget, but he had retreated into the cliché that it was better to have something to do, something to occupy his mind.

But he could not stay at work on Sundays nor through the long hours of the night. At first he had gone for aimless drives, sometimes stopping at a pub, talking to people, listening, sometimes getting drunk, until one night he found himself in the American bar of a hotel in Surrey with no idea of how he got there. He had taken a room and slept it off and returned home the following morning.

He was haunted by many things, but the most immediate and the worst was the knowledge that he had to sort out Sue's belongings and give them to a charity. He began one Sunday morning with the sun streaming into the house. It was like self-mutilation. There were dresses he knew well from times she had worn them on holiday in Corfu or the Algarve; there were shoes, there were handbags and stoles, furs—the rooms were filled with memories. He gritted his teeth and forced himself to think of each garment, each accessory, as so much cotton, silk or leather, without her personality, without her aura.

He emptied everything onto the floor of her sitting-room and soon the pile grew high. At first he had looked at each piece of clothing, felt in each pocket, but later he began to work more quickly, grabbing armfuls of underwear or dresses, scooping up shoes, throwing them on the growing pile. He had no idea she'd had so much. Drawers, dressing-tables, walk-in cupboards, wardrobes—all were full.

And then, going through the drying cupboard, where some of her underwear was still hanging, he saw at the back, a small attaché case. He pulled it out and looked at it frowning. It had belonged to his first wife, Margaret. He took it into the bedroom and opened it and immediately wished he hadn't. It held two photograph albums and a book of cuttings. He knew what they contained and decided not to look at them. But almost of their own volition his hands raised the cover of the first album.

It was worse than he had imagined it would be. It contained the pictures of his son Dick as a child, blurred photographs taken on the box Kodak. He knew them all so well because he had looked at them many times. But he saw things in them he had not seen before, little quirks of expression on the boy's face. And something else; in almost every photograph of Dick, Margaret made an appearance, holding him as a child, being with him as a boy. The second album was Dick grown up; Dick married to Lucy; Stephen born: Dick in uniform; Dick out of uniform; holidays in Wales and Scotland. Halfway through the album he knew he was never going to finish the set of books without a drink. He went down to the drawing-room but he had run out. In the kitchen he found the liquor which Sue had used for cooking. There was a bottle of Bual Madeira, one of Cyprus sherry and half a bottle of rum. He took the Madeira upstairs and began to go through the cuttings album.

They started with Dick at school winning the mile; Dick scoring fifty at cricket; Dick's poem in the school magazine;

56

then a gap and a cutting of a news picture of Dick getting his wings at the passing-out parade; Dick's marriage—and then, suddenly, the stories of the accident. CHILD CAUSES ACCIDENT TO FAMILY was the *Telegraph*'s heading. FAMILY WIPED OUT IN M-WAY SMASH said the *Mirror*.

He read the *Telegraph* story: "A stone thought to have been thrown by a child from one of the bridges over the M1 caused the deaths of three members of a family near Stevenage yesterday.

"Squadron-Leader Richard Spencer, 28, his wife, Lucy, and their son Stephen, 4, were travelling south towards London at about 5 p.m. yesterday when the car suddenly swerved onto the north-bound carriage-way and crashed into an oncoming container lorry.

"All three members of the family appear to have died instantly.

"Mr Albert Gittings, 43, of Edgbaston, the driver of the lorry, was unhurt, but was taken to hospital and treated for shock. He was later released.

"Today Mr Gittings described what happened: 'The traffic was light as I was coming towards the bridge. I saw two or three kids run off to the left. One stopped and threw something. Then this car came over from the south-bound carriage-way.

"'I remember thinking, my God, he can't see, the wind-screen's shattered.

"'There was no way I could avoid him.'

"Mrs Sheila Parsons, 62, who lives near the M1, said that she often saw children playing on the bridge.

"'I've reported the matter several times to the police but they don't seem to do anything about it. I knew something like this would happen.'

"Chief Inspector Jeffrey Round of the Hertfordshire police said they had had reports in the past of young people throwing things from bridges. They were pursuing their inquiries in the area.

"An Air Ministry spokesman described Squadron Leader Spencer as one of the most experienced pilots in the RAF."

Spencer turned the pages of the book. Most newspapers had substantially the same story.

Then came the follow-ups. The *Mail* had done a feature on juvenile vandalism on the motorways; and there had been one or two other pieces on the same lines in other papers.

A week later there had been a story in the *Express* saying that the police knew who had thrown the fatal stone. The paper described him as a "small, sturdy six-year-old" whose parents both worked and whose favourite TV programmes were the American crime series. The family had been warned, said the newspaper, that unless stricter parental control was exercised, the child would be taken into care.

And that was that. There was nothing anyone could do.

He finished the Madeira and fetched the half bottle of rum. He read on for a while and then sat back in the chair staring in front of him. The sun had long since gone and the winter afternoon brought darkness. He finished the rum and later went for the sherry.

The doorbell woke him the following morning but his head was like an anvil on which someone was beating and he ignored it. Finally it stopped and he heard footsteps going down the path to the street. He fell asleep again and this time—it was between half-past nine and ten—he was awakened by the telephone. He heard it as though in a dream and ignored it too. After a while he got up, drank a cup of coffee, left the house and went out to the Heath. It was a cold, grey morning and he was wearing only a thin cardigan. He walked past Kenwood to the Highgate ponds and then up to the *Spaniards* where he had two large whiskies. When he returned home at lunchtime Robert Calland was waiting for him in his car.

"John!" Calland said.

Spencer stopped at the gate hardly recognizing him.

"You all right?" Calland said.

"Yes."

They stared at each other for several seconds and then Calland said, "Can I come in?"

Spencer led him into the drawing-room. The curtains were still closed, there was an empty whisky bottle on the floor, and several dirty glasses. "I'm sorry I can't offer you a drink."

"That's all right. I don't want one."

"What's it all about?"

Calland looked at him in surprise. "We were worried, John."

"Worried?"

"Armstrong tried to raise you at the usual time but no one answered the bell. We phoned. No one answered the phone. Naturally we were worried."

"I was out," Spencer said.

They sat in an embarrassed silence, then Spencer suddenly had a vision of himself and his house as seen through Calland's eyes. The hung-over, unshaven, seedy man in the ill-kempt and seedy room.

"John, you're not looking after yourself," Calland said. "Isn't there someone who comes in and cleans?"

"Have you got a cigarette?" Calland gave him one and lit it. "I let her go after Sue . . . after what happened."

"It's not good being alone."

"For Christ's sake, stop worrying about me and stop nagging me! I'm all right."

"You're not all right. A blind fool could see that. The reaction's hitting you. It's taken some time but that's what's happening."

Spencer looked at Calland with fresh eyes. He saw the neat, well-groomed, after-shaved, manicured young executive. What the hell did Calland know about reactions, or behaviour, or life itself for that matter?

They talked on for a while, Spencer hardly listened. The Goddard contract was coming up, there was more trouble with the works manager in Slough. There were other decisions that had to be made. Suddenly he stood up, tired of it all and said, "I'm going away for a while. You deal with it."

A look of relief passed across Calland's face and was replaced by a more calculating expression. Was this the opportunity he was waiting for, Spencer wondered? Would he make his big push now to be rid of the "old man"? He found he did not care, could not even think about it.

59

Calland stayed, making worried noises for another ten or fifteen minutes and then Spencer watched him go down the path to the car. There was a jauntiness in his step that had not been there when he arrived. Spencer gave him a minute or two and then he went out again, this time to the *Duke of Hamilton* and had two more large whiskies. He wandered down Heath Street almost as far as Chalk Farm before turning back. When he got home he made himself an egg nogg, drank it, then brought in some twigs and a bucket of smokeless fuel from the garden shed and lit a fire in the drawing-room. He fetched the photograph albums and the cuttings albums and watched them burn. By the time they were nothing more than ash—and it took a long time for the fire to reduce them—he had come to a decision.

Twice in his lifetime his family had been taken from him—for after the crash on the motorway it could be said that Margaret's alcoholism was tantamount to death—twice people he loved had been killed. The first time there was nothing he could do: what if he had hunted for the children, what if he had found them? Could he have beaten them? Kicked them? Made them suffer as they had made others suffer? Even in his anger he had not contemplated that. But now? Now there *was* someone who could be made to pay, not only for Sue but the debt that went all the way back to Berlin. It was a question of finding Bruno.

*    *    *

At seven o'clock the following Saturday evening the doorbell rang. For a moment he was tempted to ignore it, then it occurred to him that it might be Detective Chief Superintendent Nichols.

But the man on the doorstep was of medium height and plump, almost pear-shaped. His face was round, with heavy patches under his eyes which gave him a weary look. On his head he wore a green felt Tyrolean hat with a large brown-and-orange pheasant's feather at the side. It gave him a raffish, decadent appearance, like a battered old car painted a psychedelic pattern.

"Herr Spencer?" Hearing the German accent turned Spencer's blood cold.

"Yes."

The man held out some sort of identification card, then bowed and said, "Hoest. *Kriminalpolizei*."

"What?"

"You would say Chief Superintendent. Chief Superintendent Hoest. Berlin police. Have you some minutes?"

He hesitated. "I've seen the criminal police. And the political police."

"I know," Hoest said gently. Somehow, Spencer was not quite sure how, the policeman had managed to insinuate himself between Spencer and the door-frame and was standing in the hall.

"You are going somewhere?" He was looking at a suitcase leaning against the wall.

"I'm going away."

"On holiday?"

"Sort of."

Hoest sighed gently. "It is good, I think. It will help after what happened. Where do you go?"

"Scotland," Spencer said, caught unawares, and only realized after he had said it how ridiculous it must sound— Scotland in November. "What can I do for you?"

"Perhaps we could talk for a little. Not long."

"I've got nothing to add."

"Perhaps."

"Come on then." He led the way to his study.

"A moment," Hoest said as he reached the first landing. He looked into the study. "This is where they . . ." he waggled the first and second fingers of his right hand and allowed them to represent the missing words. ". . . Riemeck?"

"Yes."

"And then they came out here; Herr Riemeck, the other man and your wife. Down the staircase. Where is the kitchen?"

"At the back."

"Yes. I understand. All I want is—geography? Is that how you say it?"

"Of the house?"

"Geography of the house." He looked about him for another few seconds. "They came out, went down the staircase, across the hall and there, at the door, he shot them."

"Yes."

"Good. Now I have the picture in my head."

They went into the study. "I was going to make myself some coffee," Spencer said.

"Coffee?" Hoest smiled gently.

"Tea, then."

"Tea is better for me." He tapped his ample belly. "Coffee is gas to me. But tea, especially English tea, I like. Do you know of Twinings tea? I buy Twinings tea in Berlin; the best, I think."

"I have Jackson's Darjeeling."

"Good. Good."

Spencer went out to make the tea, leaving Hoest alone. The Chief Superintendent walked slowly around the room, taking in the array of stereo equipment. It reminded him of rooms glimpsed in his wife's glossy magazines. He seated himself on the Chesterfield, upright, hands on knees, staring straight ahead. He seemed to be dissociating himself from his surroundings and in a sense this was true. Hoest was only truly happy at home in Berlin. He and his wife—his children were grown up—occupied one of the old pre-war apartments that had escaped the bombing, behind the Hotel Sylterhof, and if his investigations had never taken him farther west than Grunewald and farther east than the Brandenburger Tor, he would have been delighted. He had glassed in the balcony of his apartment and it was here that he grew his geraniums. Colleagues brought him cuttings from Spain and Portugal, France and Italy, and he tended them with loving care, though he admitted, even to himself, that geraniums did not need a great deal of care. That suited him very well.

But there were times when crimes were committed outside his ideal area and he was forced to travel. He had been to Stuttgart, Bonn and Munich many times and he had become used to such visits. There were also trips to foreign lands,

France for instance, and Holland, and once to Norway. He had spent a week in Oslo where it had rained incessantly and he'd had to buy an umbrella. That journey was best forgotten.

These quirks of Herr Hoest's nature often brought smiles to the faces of his colleagues, especially now that he was getting on towards retirement. He tolerated their amusement. He did not need to remind them that he had been the youngest Chief Superintendent in the history of the *Kriminalpolizei*; they knew all about that.

Spencer came back with a tray. "Milk and sugar?"

"Thank you, no."

Hoest sipped at his tea, then said, "What do they say?"

"Who?"

"Your police."

"Come now, you're not going to tell me you have to come to me for your information."

"We are in touch, naturally. But sometimes, you know, we like to keep things from each other."

"They don't seem to be any further. I mean, they don't know who the men were or why they wanted Riemeck." He thought Hoest looked relieved. Or perhaps it was simply his normal weary expression.

"I would like you to look at something."

"More pictures?"

"Just a few."

He took out his wallet and selected four photographs. The first was of a young woman, perhaps in her mid-twenties, with short black hair. She was sitting on a suitcase in what looked like a railway station. The second was the head and shoulders of a strong-jawed man with a big square face and long side-burns. The third showed a man standing in front of a lake. He was short and bald. Spencer shook his head doubtfully. "The third one, the one who was killed. That looks like him."

"Yes. His name is Tellier. Louis Tellier."

"So you know one of them?"

"Maybe. Maybe all three."

"Who was this Tellier?"

"We don't know all his background."

"What then?"

"Later, Mr Spencer. First let me ask you, have you ever seen such a thing before?"

He drew from his wallet a small piece of material and placed it on the desk. It was the same as the one Spencer had received in the post, the three heraldic leopards. He felt the blood drain away from his skin and realized that Hoest was watching him carefully. "No," he said, reaching forward and picking it up. He looked at it casually but carefully as he imagined he would have done if it had been unfamiliar. Then he turned it over and looked at the back. "Should I have seen it?"

"I do not know. That is what I am asking."

"What is it? It looks like a badge of some sort."

"Precisely."

"You sew it onto a shirt or something. Or perhaps on your sleeve. Like Boy Scouts."

Hoest smiled. "Boy Scouts? Ah, yes. No, not Boy Scouts, I think. Do you know where we found this?"

"No."

"In the Volkswagen. It was—how do you say in English?— wod-ged in two pieces of wood."

"Wedged."

"Wedged. In the wardrobe of the Volkswagen. We looked for the other but could not find it anywhere."

"What other?"

"There are always two, Mr Spencer." He picked up the cloth patch and placed it against his collar. "This one goes here, but where is the one for here?" He tapped the other side of the collar.

"Lost?"

"That is what we fear. We thought you might be able to help."

"Why me?"

"They came here, Mr Spencer. It might have dropped on your carpet; you might have picked it up."

"No, I would have told the police. Our . . . Scotland Yard, I mean."

"And you didn't. Well, that is a help by itself."

"You mean they might have kept it from you?" He was talking for the sake of talking. Trying to act normally. But his behaviour seemed enlarged, like a drunk acting sober; everything was too deliberate, too planned.

"More tea?"

"Thank you," Hoest said, shaking his head.

"What's so special about them?" Spencer asked.

"Have you heard of the *Freikorps*, Mr Spencer?"

"The what?" He could feel the tips of cold fingers touching his heart.

"*Freikorps*. Free Corps. There were several of them. During the war some of those people in the occupied lands wished to join with the German forces and fight the Russians. They formed units called *Freikorps*."

"I've heard of the Spanish Blue Division. I know they fought on the Eastern Front for the Germans against the Russians."

"No, these came from occupied countries. Do you recognize names like Joyce, Baillie-Stewart, Amery?"

"You mean William Joyce?"

"You called him Lord Haw-Haw, not so?"

"That's right. Weren't the others traitors too? Weren't they called the Radio Traitors because they broadcast anti-British propaganda from Berlin to Britain?" He could feel the sweat breaking out on his brow and under his arms and running down his rib-cage.

"That is correct. Do you know what happened to them after the war, Mr Spencer?"

"Of course."

"The English hanged them, yes?"

"That's right. But what has this got to do with the free—the *Freikorps*?"

"It was one of your people, Amery, who suggested a *Freikorps* of British—"

"But that's ridiculous. I can understand the Germans recruiting in occupied countries, but they couldn't recruit in Britain."

"Correct. But there were thousands of British and Australians and South Africans and New Zealanders in prisoner-of-war camps. That is where they recruited. Amery and one or two other sympathizers went round the camps talking to the prisoners. If they showed interest they were taken to a rest centre in Berlin, given good food, drink and women. It was like a holiday. If they were not sure, they were sent back to the camp; the difference between the rest centre and the camp was very great. Good psychology, not so? Were you not in a camp, Herr Spencer?"

"Yes."

"Where was that?"

"You know damn well where it was."

"Yes, of course, near Bremerhaven."

Spencer stared angrily at Hoest. He imagined that this was what he should be doing; in reality he felt quite different.

Hoest veered away from the dangerous area. "Do you know how many of the prisoners joined the British *Freikorps*, Herr Spencer?"

"No."

"Not more than forty. Out of all the camps, out of all the thousands of soldiers and sailors and flyers, unhappy men, prisoners, not more than forty." He looked up. "It is something to be proud of, that."

"Yes. What happened to them?"

"Some fought in the last battles in Berlin and were killed. Some deserted from the *Freikorps* and were picked up by your soldiers. Some were brought back to England and sent to prison. And some . . ." he moved his hand ". . . some were never found."

"What do you mean? Their bodies?"

"I mean that they disappeared, Herr Spencer. No one knows what happened to them or where they went. According to the camp records at Bremerhaven, you were sent to Berlin on the fourth of November, 1944. Why?"

It was so sudden that even though he had been half waiting for it, it took him by surprise.

"What are you trying to insinuate?"

"Insin—?"

"What are you getting at? What are you after?"

"The truth, Herr Spencer."

"Don't talk bloody rubbish to me! You come in here and start badgering me. You've no rights here, you know. This isn't Berlin. I don't have to answer any of your questions."

"My dear Herr Spencer, I know—"

"No, you *don't* know. This is London. England." He was on his feet now, standing over the Chief Superintendent. "I've told everything I know to the English police and if they want to ask any further questions, that's fine. But no one else, is that clear?"

"That is clear. Please, Herr Spencer, let me apologize if I have offended you. In my work I'm afraid it is often so." He climbed wearily to his feet. "But sometimes it is necessary. You see, there is an unexplained gap in your life and policemen do not like gaps. They like everything so and so, like bank managers. Forgive me."

He picked up his Tyrolean hat. "Just one—"

"No."

"Just look at this. I have come a long way to see you."

Spencer took the fourth photograph. It was blurred and seemed to have been taken with a telephoto at extreme range. It showed a man in a street about to enter the doorway of a building. It was winter, for he was wearing a heavy leather coat with a fur collar. He was a large man with thinning light hair, the ends of which had been brushed sideways over his scalp to hide his bald patch. Although his body was turning away from the camera his face was full and it seemed he was either looking down the street to see if he was being followed, or else had spotted the photographer. Spencer knew he was looking at a photograph of Bruno Gutmann.

"Let me tell you something about this man before you answer," Hoest said. "In Germany we have two kinds of terrorism. You may call one political terrorism and the other criminal terrorism. You must have heard of the Baader-Meinhoff gang: Gudrun Enslin and Jan-Carl Raspe, Holger Meins, Irmgard Moller . . ."

"Some."

"These are political terrorists who burn stores and rob banks and kill people to make a more beautiful world. And they are helped all over Germany by what we call there the *schili*: what you perhaps call the chic Left. Middle-class left-wing people with money who want the thrill of associating with terrorists.

"They have supplied a network of couriers and safe-houses all over Germany where the terrorists can hide. They also supply them with money, clothes, cars. Naturally this makes our job very difficult. Now say to yourself, Herr Spencer: what if ordinary criminals could be looked after by such a group of people? They, too, rob banks and kill people but they have nowhere to run, nowhere to hide. Would it not be nice if a whole section of the population sympathized with them and hid them and looked after them and gave them money and cars. Heaven, not so? The promised land! Well, that is what this man thought. As long ago as 1969 he organized the bombing of a store in Cologne and killed six people. It gave him credibleness—is that the word?"

"Credibility."

"*Ja*. Credibility as a terrorist among the *schili*. In 1972 in Hanover he burnt another store. This time three people were dead. His gang has robbed banks in Hamburg, Dortmund and Munich and possibly Bremen, but we are not sure. We think four, we are sure of three. And in these robberies two people were shot dead. You see, we have known about this man—he uses many names now—for a long time."

"You're going too fast," Spencer said. "You mean he's not a political terrorist. That he bombed and killed—"

"So that it would *appear* so. To give himself a terrorist background," Hoest said. "This is not so strange. Many young people start off by being 'political'. They rob and kill, they claim, for 'political' reasons. But then they become used to it. They become used to having money they did not earn, of riding in Mercedes cars they did not buy. It is corrupting, *ja*? We know it has happened in Germany and in Italy and France too. Many of the kidnap gangs started out as 'politicals'. Now it is their way of life."

"And this man is a criminal?" Spencer said, indicating the picture.

"Purely criminal. We know very little about him. We know that before he operated in the West he was in the Eastern zone and we know he spent some years in the early sixties in England.

"For a long time his gang did what they liked. When they robbed, some of the *schili* took them in, hid them, moved them, looked after them. In such circumstances it is almost impossible to trace them. But then, about four months ago we had some luck.

"For a long time we had been trying to infiltrate our people into the terrorist underground. One of them made contact with this man. He spent nearly two months with the group, but they discovered who he was and they killed him. They killed him here in your house, Herr Spencer."

"Riemeck?"

"Just so."

"But what was he doing in England?"

"Checking on this man." He tapped the picture.

"And why did they torture him?"

"We think to find out what he had already passed on about them."

"Had he passed on anything?"

"Very little. He was only beginning to gain their confidence. You see, what we really wanted to know was where their headquarters are. Most of the time they are living somewhere ordinary, spending their money, having a good time. Then they rob a bank and for months they are in hiding. If we knew where their base was we would have a chance of catching them. Do you understand?"

Spencer said nothing.

"Listen to me," Hoest said. "You have become mixed up in something very complex. I want to warn you that anything can happen. Just as it happened here in this house. I don't want to open the trunk of a car one day and see your dead body. Now, look closely at the photograph."

Spencer looked and then shook his head. "No, I've never seen him before."

That night he lay awake for a long time. What did it amount to? They had found the collar patch in the Volkswagen but there was nothing to connect him with that since he had long ago destroyed the other one. It must have been identified in Berlin; no ordinary person—and that included the German police—would have been familiar with so recondite an organization as the British Free Corps. After it had been identified, Hoest had done some research on the whole question of the Free Corps. Hoest knew, because Spencer had told both the British and German police, that he had been a prisoner of war in Germany. Spencer had not mentioned Berlin. But Hoest knew he had been sent there? Would he be digging in Berlin?

If he had told Hoest the whole truth the German police would have had a reasonable chance of finding Bruno but even as he considered such a thing his body twisted and turned in protest. His whole life had been devoted to keeping the secret, to blotting it out, living as though it had never happened. He had never mentioned it to Margaret and sometimes he wondered if that was the reason, when their family was wiped out, they had nothing left to give each other. Had he built a wall around himself to hide behind? And he had never told Sue. Being so much younger she was doubly or trebly removed from the meaning of his action, but his shame had always held him back. And this was why he had to deal with Bruno; there was no one else who could help him and when one finally worked things out, everything came back to Bruno.

\*　　\*　　\*

"Not the entire German Army, not the whole of the Reich, not the Führer himself knows what to do with him!" Bruno said, laughing. "We can overcome the world, but what to do with John Spencer?"

"I'm sure it cannot be so difficult as that," Mrs Gutmann said. "You always exaggerate."

70

The year was 1944, the place was a house in Graf Spee-strasse, just off the Tiergarten in Berlin. It was a much grander house than any Spencer had been in before, even though some of the walls were cracked and wooden beams held up the ceiling.

"From the bombs," Bruno explained.

"Your British bombs," Mrs Gutmann said, severely.

"Not *his* any more, mother, he's one of us now." He caught Spencer by the arm and took him to the window. "Look," he said. "They cannot hit us." A house across from the Gutmanns' villa was a pile of rubble, others had been damaged and trees more or less severely splintered. Spencer turned back into the room. It was on the ground floor of the house, large and well-proportioned, and if it hadn't been for the baulks of timber shoring up the moulded ceiling, it would have been elegant. It was packed with furniture, heavy black oak chairs and cup-boards, three clocks, one a long-case, the others wall clocks, one of which was inlaid with mother-of-pearl; heavy maroon velvet black-out curtains. By the door stood a bucket of sand, one of water, and a stirrup-pump. Around the walls were heavily-framed portraits in the Van Dyck manner. After he had been in the house a few days he learnt why this room was so packed. A bomb, which had demolished one of the nearby houses, had made the dining-room unsafe so all its furniture had been brought into the drawing-room.

"Take him up and show him his sleeping place," Mrs Gutmann said.

"Come on, Johnnie," Bruno said, "follow me." He bounded up the stairs. "We're sharing, isn't it?" he said, as they reached the landing. His English was good but Spencer noticed every now and then he used a phrase which didn't fit.

It was a fair-sized bedroom with two beds, a dressing-table, chest-of-drawers, an old-fashioned wash-stand with basin and jug, and an enormous double wardrobe. One wall was domin-ated by a lithograph of Hitler framed by two Nazi flags. There was a cluster of photographs on another wall grouped around a second portrait. To Spencer the face was almost as familiar as that of Hitler. A similar portrait had hung on the wall of their sitting-room in Bromley.

Bruno pointed at the second portrait. "You know who that is?"

Spencer nodded. "Sir Oswald Mosley."

"Ahh . . ."

"We had one like it. My father is a Blackshirt."

"What!"

"He used to march in the East End of London."

"That's incredible! You really are one of us! Look, that's my father there." He pointed to a photograph of a British Union of Fascists East End rally. Mosley, in his black shirt and armband, was talking into a microphone. Bruno indicated a figure seated on the platform to his left. "My father, Lionel Boyse. That's my real name: Boyse. But we have taken my mother's family name now. My father was on the executive. Just think, your father and my father might have been in the same crowd."

As they looked at the photographs he put his arm around Spencer's shoulder. "You'll like it here, Johnnie. You're safe now."

Spencer said nothing. He was somewhat confused by his own motives. He had hated the fascist movement in Britain and had been ashamed of his father. Now he was identifying with them. He could not rationalize his position—sixteen was too young—he only knew that the fear and despair of the past five months were beginning to fade.

"I've got something to show you," Bruno said. "Sit down. Sit on the bed. *Your* bed." He reached up onto the top of the great wardrobe, pulled down a square flat cardboard box and opened it. Spencer could see a field-grey uniform jacket. Bruno began to put it on. Spencer sat on his own bed—so different from the hard bunk of boards which he had been used to—next to his small parcel of belongings which were all that had been saved when the ship went down, and watched.

Bruno, Spencer was later to learn, was nineteen years old, three years older than he, and was large, fair-haired, pink-skinned and somewhat plump. He had blond eye-brows and pale blue eyes and in some lights this gave him almost a sinister appearance. His hands, as he did up the buttons, were delicate and chubby. When he had finished he looked at himself in the wardrobe mirror and turned, very slowly.

"Isn't it beautiful?" he said. "Waffen S.S. uniform but you see they've taken all the insignia off. Now look." He pulled from one pocket a Union Jack armband and slipped it on. "And these go here," he said. He took out two patches and held them up to his collar, where they would eventually be sewn. It was the first time Spencer had ever seen the patches with the three heraldic leopards. "You'll have a uniform, too, Johnnie, we must see to it. Oh. And here. On the cuff. This must be sewn on the cuff." He held up another patch. This had gothic lettering on it which read: BRITISH FREE CORPS.

"There are Norwegian, Dutch, French, Swedish, even Spanish units. Now we're going to have a British one to fight the Russians. That's what you want, isn't it? To fight the Russians?"

"Yes."

"We're all brothers, you know. The Germans and us. I think of myself as an Englishman really. Why should we be fighting each other? The Führer has always said he cannot understand why Britain and Germany should be at war when the common enemy is Russia."

"Bruno!" The call came from downstairs.

"You want to wash your hands?" Bruno said. "Then we will eat."

They ate in the kitchen at the rear of the house and here, too, if he looked from the window, Spencer could see the piles of rubble where the bombs had hit. They ate a cabbage soup with dumplings; he could taste occasional minute pieces of meat and after what he had been used to it was like a banquet. Mrs Gutmann followed his eyes to the window. "We are next," she said. "They bomb us every night, your people. How can we escape?"

"Not *his* people, mother," Bruno burst out. "I told you he's one of us. His father is a Blackshirt. He may even have known Daddy." Mrs Gutmann was a female version of Bruno, slightly above medium height and big-boned, with flaxen hair and a broad pink face with high cheek bones.

"Did you go to the rallies?"

"Once."

"I did," Bruno said. "On my father's shoulder."

"My father went," Spencer said, remembering the short, angry man who would come home on a winter Saturday evening, with his clothes torn, sometimes with livid weals on his face.

"My husband was political," Mrs Gutmann said.

"Sir Oswald Mosley was the natural leader of England," Bruno said. "There would have been none of this," he waved his hand to indicate the war, "if he had been in charge."

A tall and rather stooping man came down the stairs and into the kitchen. He looked at Bruno, smiled and raised his hand and said, *"Heil Hitler!"*

"Don't be funny," Bruno said. "You can get into trouble for that." A look which Spencer had not seen before crossed his face: it was petulant and vicious.

"The uniform, Bruno. I was saluting the uniform. Isn't that why you dress up?"

"He's always dressing up," Mrs Gutmann said. "This is another one." She indicated Spencer.

"You've come to fight the Russians too, have you?"

"Yes."

"That's a relief," the man said, taking his place at the table. Though the expression was mocking, his eyes were not unkind. But Spencer felt uncomfortable.

"This is Mr Lange," Bruno said. "He comes from Africa."

"Where did you spring from?" Lange said to Spencer, as he began his soup.

Before he could answer, Bruno said, "He's only sixteen and already he's been torpedoed, isn't it, Johnnie?"

He made Spencer seem almost glamorous: the torpedoing on the North Atlantic convoy, sole survivor of his ship, picked up by the U-boat that had done the damage. The weeks aboard the *Heide*, then the months in the camp near Bremerhaven. It had sounded romantic the way he told it. As Spencer listened it was as though Bruno was describing someone else: a young Siegfried, perhaps, gone out to conquer the world.

The frugal meal came to an end. Lange said, "And how many of you gallant Britishers have joined this . . . what's it called? Free Corps?"

Mrs Gutmann said: "Always dressing up. How he expects me to keep up with the washing and ironing I can't tell. Hours in front of the mirror up there in his room; first his father's old uniform from England, now this one."

"Well, I must say I feel relieved that when the Russians break through the eastern perimeter Mr Spencer here will be at the barricades," Lange said.

"The Russians will never break through," Bruno said. "Never. The Führer has said there are weapons that will . . ."

"Ah, the secret weapons," Lange said. "They are going to bring England to her knees. I wonder whose bombs these are that keep falling on our heads." He finished his meal and opened a small bottle of pills.

"I'll get your water, Norbert," Mrs Gutmann said, going to the tap. "How is your stomach today?"

"Much better now that I know I'll be safe."

"You're being very funny," Bruno said. "I'm warning you, you can get into trouble for saying things like this." He was staring angrily at Lange. There was a sudden silence. Even Lange looked uncomfortable. He threw two white pills into the back of his mouth and drank some water. Then he rose and left the table.

Spencer never got to know Lange very well. He saw him at meal times, which they always took in the kitchen, and sometimes on the stairs or coming out of the bathroom. But slowly he put together his biography. He knew that Lange worked in the *Rundfunk* editing copy that went out on the English Broadcast Service. He knew that he came from the old German colony of South-West Africa, that he had been lecturing at a University in Germany when war broke out, and that he boarded with Mrs Gutmann just as he, Spencer, boarded there, except that Spencer's fees were being paid by the Foreign Office. And though it was clear that Mrs Gutmann was several years older than Lange, it was also clear that she had her eye on him.

After that first meal Bruno took him for a walk. He had seen some of the bombing around the Zoo Station on his arrival that morning but had been too confused to take it in. Now, as they walked along the edge of the Tiergarten, down towards the canal and into Kurfurstenstrasse, he could see the devastation. Whole streets seemed to lie in ruins. In the Wittenbergplatz they found an old man circling a letterbox trying to insert his letter.

"You cannot do it," Bruno said to him.

"What? Can't post a letter? You're mad!"

Bruno shrugged and the two walked on. "They closed the post boxes to save petrol collecting the mail. A good thing, too, it doesn't hurt anyone to walk to the post office. Leave the old fool, he knows so much."

They turned and began to walk back towards Graf Spee-strasse. Bruno was in his uniform and drew curious and sometimes admiring glances. He carried himself very straight.

"Don't let Lange upset you," he said. "The Führer has said that next month the Allies will suffer the greatest defeat in their history." The streets were getting dark now and they were walking along the deserted banks of the canal. Bruno took Spencer's arm. "The Führer has said there is a new secret weapon so powerful that England will be plunged into *chaos*. She will not be able to emerge without Germany's help. Then in April next year we will use our whole strength against Russia. In fifteen months she will be in our hands. We will eradicate Communism and clear out the Jews. In the summer of 1946 German U-boats will be equipped with a new secret weapon that will destroy the British and American navies. By September Japan will rule China, Australia and South East Asia and under German leadership, Europe will enter a new era."

•   •   •   •   •

76

Spencer awoke late to a cold but sunny Sunday morning in Hampstead. He finished his packing, made himself a light meal, ordered a taxi for half-past six that evening and went out to buy the newspapers. He walked past Christchurch and into Hampstead Square. The inchoate rage of the past weeks had changed to a cold, controlled anger and now he was icy calm. He seemed to be two people, the first walking through the morning sunshine; the second watching the first. A woman tourist was taking photographs of the Queen Anne houses. He went on down to the newspaper seller at the Underground station, bought the papers, then walked up Heath Street, turned up the Hollybush steps and went into the tiny bar of the *Hollybush* itself. He ordered a pint of bitter and took it outside. It was warm in the sun and several others had brought their pints out too. It was the sort of convivial Sunday morning that he and Sue had enjoyed. He felt the rage build up again and fought to regain the earlier control. What he was about to do needed the chill of uninvolvement.

He sipped his bitter and read the headlines and a feeling of being watched came over him. He looked up but the only new arrival was the lady tourist, taking pictures of the bijou houses off the Hollybush steps and then of the groups of drinkers outside the pub itself. Spencer and the rest were eventually going to find themselves in a stranger's snap album. He wondered where he'd end up; she looked American and seemed to be using the camera with a certain ease. Being the owner of two expensive cameras he looked at hers with mild interest. It was an East German Praktica. She took a few more pictures, then turned and went down the steps.

He had a second pint, left the *Hollybush* and walked into Cannon Place, but on impulse decided not to go into his house. Instead he walked on and came to the Heath. It was alive with families taking the chance of sunshine. He walked up towards Kenwood, wishing that the time would pass, wishing that he could get going, and reached the great house just as the doors were opened to the public. Again he felt the sensation that someone was watching him. He stopped, turned, and heard the click of the shutter even before he saw her. This time she spoke.

"May I speak with you?" she said. The accent was German.

"Me?"

"Yes, Mr Spencer."

He looked at her more closely. She was in her mid-thirties, thin, but well-proportioned, with black hair cut in a fringe and an attractive angular face. She wore a blue suede coat over long, slender legs. There was something fresh about her. It was the same quality that Sue had had. Perhaps it was the colouring. For a second it almost seemed to him she *was* Sue. Again he fought to regain control; again he almost lost.

"Who are you?" he said.

A queue was forming at the door and he moved away to the lawn.

"My name is Lilo Essenbach."

"You've been taking pictures of me?"

"I hope you are not offended."

"Why?"

"I'm from *Der Spiegel*," she said, "I want to do a story on you."

"Why didn't you ring me?"

"In case you said no."

"You followed me this morning."

"You live here, I wanted pictures against your own background."

"I don't like being spied on."

"I wasn't spying. I was open. You saw me in the street and at the bar. I did not hide."

"Why do you want to do a story?"

"You can ask that?"

"I don't see journalists." He thought of the days and especially the nights when the telephone had scarcely stopped ringing; when the street outside was thick with them.

She stopped and turned towards him and he saw there was anxiety in her dark brown eyes. "It will be a good story. I do not want to make trouble for you. You will like the story."

"I'm sorry."

"But why not?"

"There have been enough stories written."

"I've come a long way to see you."

There was something familiar about the phrase, someone else had used it recently, but out of the mass of people who had talked to him he could not isolate the individual.

"I'm sorry," he repeated. "Anyway, I'm going away. You must excuse me."

The anxiety had given way to anger. "If I write a story and do not speak with you it will be a bad story."

"Write what you damn well please," he said, and walked swiftly away.

*       *       *

Liverpool Street Station at seven o'clock on a Sunday evening was almost deserted. It was a depressing, dirty place, and only a handful of people were standing at the barrier to the boat train. He had booked through to Berlin, but instead of taking his seat in the first-class compartment, he went into the buffet car and ordered a meal. It was called "Traveller's Fayre", a bowl of tinned soup, a grey sirloin steak that appeared to have come straight from the deep freeze to a microwave oven, and packet cheese. By the time he was on his second cup of coffee the train was pulling into Harwich.

The *Königin Wilhelmina* was at Parkstone Quay and there was no body search or luggage inspection as they went aboard. This was precisely why he had decided to travel by train rather than by air. He had a cabin to himself and he stood in it for a moment wondering whether he should hide the pistol. But he was wearing a heavy sheepskin jacket, itself so bulky that the outline of the gun did not show. He went on deck and stood in the cold and looked at the misty lights of Harwich and watched the passengers as they moved about the upstairs bars and lounges. There were very few and he recognized no one. He had a drink at the bar and soon after the ship sailed he went to his bunk.

This was a time he always hated: being alone in the bowels of a ship again. He lay rigidly, listening to the thump-thump of the screw churning in the water, feeling the vibrations of the shaft, and his thoughts went back to the convoy and the shattering roar of the exploding torpedoes.

This was something Bruno had always mentioned, the fact that Spencer had been torpedoed. He had told his mother and Lange that first day. Spencer remembered being taken to the house in Charlottenburg to meet Astley and Richards, and again it was almost the first thing that Bruno had said. It was as though he gained some sort of reflected glory. But neither Astley nor Richards had been much impressed. They were an unbalanced, dangerous couple.

There had been several houses for the Free Corps volunteers at that time in Berlin. One he knew was in Grunewald, but he had never been there, only to the house in Charlottenburg. Bruno had taken him there one evening at the end of his first week in Berlin, "to meet some of the chaps". Bruno brought out phrases like that in English but often now when he was at home he spoke German to his mother and Lange; Spencer was picking it up rapidly.

"This is where they wanted to send you," Bruno said, as they made their way through the rubble-choked streets. There had been a raid the previous evening and wires still hung down onto the pavements and small fires smouldered in some of the buildings. They passed a small lake glinting in the starlight. "But the house is not ready yet."

This was a lie. Although only two floors were habitable there were at least three vacant bedrooms, any one of which Spencer could have had. It was only later he realized that Mrs Gutmann was being paid by the German Foreign Office to keep him.

If he had been expecting a welcome from his fellow-countrymen he was disappointed. Both Astley and Richards viewed him with suspicion, which wasn't helped by Bruno, who immediately started telling them how Spencer had been torpedoed.

The house was luxurious after the camp: iron bedsteads in the rooms, carpets on the floors and in the passages. There was also a common-room with several easy chairs, a newspaper and magazine rack, and two writing tables. Around the walls were large pictures of Hitler, Mussolini and Goering.

Richards was a small man with a pale skin and blue-black jowl. He had been a motor mechanic in peace-time and seemed to have absorbed some of the grime and grease of the garage. He was nervous and highly-strung and his movements were jerky. He offered no greeting when Spencer was brought into the room and he stopped with his pen poised above the paper and said, "Have you studied National Socialism?" which he pronounced "socialismus".

"No," Spencer said.

He opened a drawer and took out a copy of *Mein Kampf.* "Here, read this. Make it your Bible. You will be asked about it." He spoke with nervous authority. Later that evening Spencer asked him where he came from and Richards replied, "Where we come from doesn't matter. That world is finished. What is important is where we are going."

Astley, by comparison, was tall and fair-skinned with curious slanting eyes and Spencer learned he had been a first class tennis player. He had little conversation except sport. It was clear that he had never done as well as he thought he deserved. He had never, for instance, got beyond the first round at Wimbledon. He blamed the Jews for this. "They make fortunes out of sport," he said, "while we starve. But here they know about sport, they know how important it is."

Later two girls arrived and they all went to a *nachtlokaal* a couple of streets away. It was filled with soldiers home on leave and they had difficulty in finding a place to sit. The air was thick with smoke and the band played loudly. Astley and Richards drank schnapps with beer chasers and they were soon half drunk and pawing the girls, who didn't seem to mind. Bruno watched them with mild amusement but in his eyes was a calculating look.

"We'll have to get Spencer a girl," Astley said. "Why don't you see to that, Bruno? Bruno knows where to get the girls." The four of them began to dance, leaving Bruno and Spencer at the table. Bruno put his hand on Spencer's arm and said, "Have you ever had a woman?"

"No."

"Do you want one? I can get you one."

"No."

Bruno smiled at him. "You and I, Johnnie. We don't need anyone."

All four were in uniform. It was the first time Spencer had worn his and the Union Jack armbands were drawing hostile glances from the soldiers. As the evening wore on Astley and Richards got drunker and their behaviour correspondingly more gross. About ten o'clock they left. By that time the hostility had permeated the room and there were jeers and catcalls as they went out of the door.

Outside they separated, Astley, Richards and the two girls going back to the house, while Bruno and Spencer began the long walk home, for the trams and the S-bahn were on restricted service and had stopped for the night. They had not got more than half way when they were caught in a raid. They ran for the shelter at the Zoo Station. The place was in uproar. Some trains were trying to get away into the suburbs before the bombing began. People were fighting their way into the compartments, trampling over anyone who got in their way.

"Cowards!" Bruno said.

Later, Spencer was to discover that these were refugees from the East who were trying to get still farther out of the path of the advancing Russians. Apart from the refugees there were hundreds of soldiers simply squatting on the platform unable to return to the front because of the transport chaos. The shelter was crammed. On one wall was a poster with pictures of an officer and three soldiers who had been shot for looting. Under the pictures the caption read: "These sentences were pronounced in the name of the German people but also in the name of those women whose husbands, brothers and sons are worthily defending the Fatherland."

The bombs were falling on the centre of the city and several explosions sounded close enough to be in the Zoological Gardens, next to the station. "Come, be comfortable," Bruno said. They lay on the floor and he put his greatcoat over them both; it was bitterly cold. Spencer slept, waking only once during the early morning. Bruno's arm was over him, protecting him and keeping him warm. He felt grateful.

About half past seven they left the shelter. "I have things to do," Bruno said. "I see you at home."

Spencer felt embarrassed in his uniform. Some people stared at him, some even saluted. Suddenly ahead of him in Budapesterstrasse there was a loud explosion. He ran forward and found that a delayed-action mine had exploded and caused a curious and macabre incident. Going up the street at that time had been a dray owned by the Schultheiss brewery. Because of the scarcity of horses the dray was being drawn by two matched white oxen. These had been almost level with the mine when it had exploded. Both oxen had been hideously disfigured. One had had its back legs blown off and was lying on a bed of its own entrails, bellowing with fright and pain. The second was simply a body. Its head, horns and part of its neck had been cleanly severed and the head now lay upright on the pavement, the large purple tongue lolling out.

A crowd collected as the dust from the mine settled and stared at the bloodstained white skins of the bullocks. The driver lay dead on the pavement, the road was running with foaming golden beer. The crowd was silent; even people used to the horrors of the bombing had never seen anything quite like this. Spencer, near the front of the crowd, felt his gorge rise and he turned away in case he vomited. It was then that someone saw his Union Jack armband. He heard a shout and felt a blow on his side. Then there were other blows, other shouts, and he was down on the ground and feet were kicking him.

Two things saved him: the crowd's rage was so great it defeated itself, it was too eager to savage him and most of its blows and kicks missed. The second was the arrival of two policemen. They were armed with carbines and wore steel helmets and quickly restored order. He was hauled to his feet and before he had come completely to his senses he found himself in the cells of a nearby police station.

At first his story was received with incredulity. The very idea of raising a pro-German British contingent smacked of fantasy. But he persisted. He made them look carefully at the field-grey uniform and they had to acknowledge that it was

Waffen S.S. They said they would check. At half-past four Lange came to fetch him. They had given him no food in the police station and he had not eaten since the previous evening. Neither Mrs Gutmann nor Bruno was at home. Lange gave him soup and black bread and sat down at the kitchen table with him, smoked a cigarette and watched him eat. He sat in silence for some time before saying, "Berlin's no place for you. God knows, the war's no place for you. How old are you?"

"Sixteen."

Lange shook his head in wonderment. "When I was sixteen all I thought about was rugby. I wasn't very good at it but we used to play it on the hard-baked fields in Windhuk. Rugby and girls and books. Those are the things you're supposed to think about when you're sixteen. Not torpedoes and guns. Do you know what they'll call you?"

"How do you mean?"

"When the war's over. And don't make any mistake about it, we've lost."

Spencer did not want him to answer his own original question. He knew what the word was, but he didn't want Lange to say it.

"Can't you go back to where you came from?" Lange said.

He thought of the big stoker, Campbell, and shook his head.

"Well, that's too bad."

Spencer ate his soup and his black bread and Lange watched him. "Let me give you a piece of advice," he said. "Don't sign your name to anything and don't have your photograph taken. Have you got a story?"

"How do you mean?"

"Use your brain, Spencer. You know as well as I do what you're doing, and when the Allies arrive in Berlin, they're going to want to know what you've been doing. There'll be a gap in your life. So think of a story. Nothing complicated. Keep it simple."

Spencer felt cold in his bowels at the inevitability of what was going to happen.

"They told you you were going to fight the Russians. A hero. Let me tell you what it's really all about. No one expects the

84

British Free Corps to fight the Russians and if it did it wouldn't make any difference. Why do you think they make you wear the Union Jack armband? Why do you think they supply members of the Free Corps with women and liquor? Because they like you? You've heard of something called morale, haven't you? Well, morale in Germany is not very high at the moment. Somehow the authorities have got to persuade the last ounce of fight out of the German people and one way is to show them that the British are not so invincible after all. They *want* you to get drunk in public; they *want* you to be seen with the local whores. That way the Germans can despise you and feel superior. Do you understand?"

It was too subtle for Spencer to understand immediately. But he thought of the advice about not signing his name and not having his photograph taken in his nice new uniform. "Yes, I understand."

Lange stubbed out a cigarette and got to his feet. "I must go to work. You'll be all right now." He stopped at the door and turned. "One more thing," he paused. "Be careful of Bruno." He opened the door and Spencer heard him go down the hall.

Spencer washed his dishes and put them away and then went up to the room he shared with Bruno. He was exhausted. He took off his uniform, folded it neatly and put it in the brown cardboard box Bruno had given him. He stood on a chair and stretched to place it on top of the huge oak wardrobe that dominated the room. He pushed it too hard for it slithered across and fell down between the wardrobe and the wall. He tugged at one corner of the wardrobe, but it was heavy. He managed to get both hands behind it and heaved with all his strength. It shifted slightly. He heaved again and it moved a few more inches. The box containing his uniform slipped down the wall and landed on the floor. He stretched as far as he could but his arm was not long enough. He pulled the wardrobe out a little farther and finally managed to close his fingers on the box. But it seemed stuck. He pulled hard and brought with it a second box; a shoe-box covered in dust and finger-marks. The house was quiet, the black-out curtains were drawn and the bedside lamp was on. He stood listening for a moment but there were only the sounds of the city. He opened the lid of the box. He was surprised by what it contained. There were four or five pairs of gold-rimmed pince-nez spectacles, a dozen or more gold wedding and signet rings, some inlaid with diamonds. There were gold bangles with precious stones, several pairs of ear-rings, two necklaces and a gold-topped fountain pen and pencil set. He stood staring at the objects for a few moments and then closed the box, put it on the floor at the back of the wardrobe where it lived in the dust, and pushed the wardrobe back into its original position. He lay on his bed trying to fathom out what he had found and finally came to the conclusion that they were the Gutmanns' family treasures hidden away for safe-keeping in the bombing. But why so many pairs of spectacles?

He heard the front door open and pretended to be asleep. Bruno came up into the room and Spencer felt him standing over the bed looking down. He kept his eyes shut and tried to breathe evenly and after a moment or two Bruno left. Spencer lay awake for a long time and when he finally fell asleep he dreamed of the blood-stained carcasses of white oxen.

*     *     *

They had left the clear, frosty weather in England and the *Königin Wilhelmina* tied up at the Hook of Holland on a grey morning with a bitter east wind blowing off the Delta. Customs was a formality and again there were no searches. The trains were waiting in the station beyond the customs shed. The Scandinavian Express was at platform three, the Berlin section at the front. Except for one or two American army personnel returning to bases in Germany the four Berlin coaches were deserted. He found his first-class compartment, put his luggage aboard and sat staring out at the raw morning.

The Rheingold Express left, and then it was the Scandinavian Express's turn and the Dutch station announcer wished its passengers a happy journey. Spencer went into the buffet car and had coffee and rolls and stared out at the achingly neat Dutch back gardens as they went through the outskirts of

Rotterdam. If he had thought about it at all he would have assumed that a journey from the Hook of Holland to Berlin would have called for one of the more important European trains, but it soon split, the bulk of it going off towards Denmark, leaving four carriages to chug into Germany. In effect, it became a local. People were getting on and off at each small station and he knew that sooner or later he would have to share the compartment. He also knew that sometime in the early afternoon the train would start crossing East Germany and that East German police and customs officials would come aboard.

The compartment was devoid of hiding places except for the areas under the seats which would be the first place any policeman would look. But at last he found somewhere he could hide his gun. He was sitting in a window-seat and he pushed the pistol underneath the white headrest cover and lodged it between the seat and the outer wall of the train where it was hidden and did not make a bulge. He had barely finished when he heard the door of the compartment slide back. He looked up and saw the woman journalist who had tried to interview him in the grounds of Kenwood House the day before.

"You do not seem pleased to see me," she said.

In a curious way he was. At least she was company.

"How did you find me?"

"I followed you."

He thought of the train at Liverpool Street and then the boat; he could have sworn she was not a passenger. He had been careful, but clearly not careful enough.

"Why?"

"I told you."

"And I told you—"

"I lied to you yesterday. I'm not from *Der Spiegel*."

"I wondered when I saw the camera. It's not professional."

"I'm a free-lance. A story like this could mean a lot to me."

"I'm sorry. I told you before."

"It has already cost me a lot."

"That's not my fault."

"I could write a story now. Just a few paragraphs and sell it to *Bild*."

"They'd never use it."

"Don't you understand, you are news! I can get off at the next station and telephone them. That's all. When you reach Berlin their reporters are at the station. Is that what you wish? And the police. They will read the story. Everyone will want to know why is Mr Spencer coming to Berlin after what happened to him and his wife? I, too, would like to know."

"That's my business."

"If I send this story you will never be allowed to do what you want to do. But let me be with you a few days. Let me talk with you. Perhaps take some more photographs. Then when you have done what you have come to do in Berlin, and gone away again, only then will I write the story."

There was something appealing about her. Something almost wistful about the angular face. What she said was true enough and he recognized it. If she wrote the sort of story she was threatening to write he would have the daily press down on him—plus Hoest. And this time the Chief Superintendent would be in his own territory. The questions would be sharper, more pointed. He would want to know what had happened in Berlin. He would want to know all kinds of things. Again Spencer felt an iciness in his bowels.

But at the same time came another thought. She was a journalist. She had contacts. Maybe he could turn that to his advantage. She was planning to use him; he might be able to use her.

"What do you want to know?" he said.

He saw her relax and lean back in her seat. "We can go slowly," she said. "We have a whole day on this train. Will you smoke?" She took a packet of thin cheroots from her bag.

He pointed to the sign on the window which indicated a non-smoking compartment.

"Do you never break rules?"

"Sometimes."

"Do you mind?"

He reached forward and took one. "What about some coffee?"

"There is no buffet car until Hanover now."

He felt some of the tension begin to seep away. "Where do you want to start?"

She looked confused. "Start?"

"Don't you have a notebook?"

"Yes, of course." She drew one out of her bag.

"Well?"

"I think we had better make a biography," she said, and then she smiled. She had particularly nice teeth, white and even, and they glistened against the heavy red of her lips. "Unless you have anything you do not wish to tell me."

"Why do you say that?"

"With most people there is something. There are places where I would lie."

"Ask your questions. We'll see."

He began to talk, slowly at first, picking the words, editing everything, but after a while he noticed she had stopped writing things down and he became somewhat less inhibited. The train drove on into the grey day. Neat, heavily-populated Holland gave way to a slightly more shaggy, more rural Germany at Bentheim. By lunch they were in Hanover waiting to be coupled to the Berlin express.

They left the train and walked up and down the platform. In the months since Sue's death Spencer had hardly spoken to anyone but the police or his colleagues at work. Now he had spent a whole morning talking to a strange woman and he realized he was feeling less tense than he had for a long time. "I've said enough about myself for the moment. What about you? Tell me about yourself."

"Me? I'm afraid that is very boring."

"You've had me talking for hours."

"But that is fascinating."

"Anyone's life is fascinating if you dig. Let me ask the questions, 'make a biography' as you put it."

"Is that not how you say it?"

"Of course it is." She smiled again and he felt a sudden warmth. "All right. Birth. When were you born?"

"Ladies do not like talking of such things."

"Let me guess then. You're twenty-eight," he said, subtracting seven years from his original estimate.

"You are very kind. I must confess more."

"Where?"

"Berlin." Slowly, too, her background emerged. The daughter of an officer in the *Schutzpolizei*. "We were a police family. My father. My uncle, My grandfather." As she spoke her mouth turned slightly downwards and a bitter expression crossed her face, she looked suddenly older. She talked of her childhood in Berlin. She had been born, it transpired, the year war had ended and remembered nothing of the early post-war days. She had been part of the West German "miracle".

Just then the Berlin train came into the station and their four coaches were coupled up.

"What about lunch?" he said, and they went to the Mitropa and had venison goulasch and a bottle of Piesporter. Over coffee he returned to the subject of the boom years and suddenly she said, "You get nothing for nothing."

"What do you mean?"

"I mean that you must pay for a miracle. And when you pay you ask yourself was it worth it? You are one of the few people outside Germany to be affected by such a payment. You lost your wife. Here in Germany it is not so rare: our judges are killed, our businessmen must have bodyguards and go to work by different routes every day. In Bonn our parliament is guarded by tanks, in the streets where our politicians live there are armoured cars. You must ask yourself, Mr Spencer, what is better: to have a little lower standard of living, but no terrorism, or be like us."

They talked on at some length. She was bitter and angry and after a while she told him why.

"You remember in 1971 when the Japanese commando came to Tegel?"

At first her choice of words confused him and then he began

90

to remember. "Japanese terrorists. They took over the airport, didn't they?"

"For nearly twenty hours. There were six of them and they took four hostages. They wanted the release of two Palestinians and two other Japanese from another terrorist attack. They said they would give the German authorities twelve hours to make ready a plane and bring the terrorists. The authorities said no. The terrorists said they would shoot one of the hostages. The Government said they did not deal with terrorists. So they shot a hostage. My father."

"Good God!"

"Yes. Like your wife, Mr Spencer. They just shot him. They made him kneel down and shot him in the back of the head. I know this because the other hostages saw it."

"They got away, didn't they?"

"Oh, yes. That was enough for the Government. They gave the plane and released the prisoners and they all flew to Libya."

The train began to slow down. "We are at the border," she said. They entered the bleak station at Marieborn; no one got off.

"We must go to the compartment," Lilo said.

He stood in the corridor. The station was surrounded by high barbed-wire fences. The East German border police in their grey uniforms walked slowly up and down the train. Several held Alsatians, some looked under the coaches; finally they came aboard and the train pulled out into East Germany.

He went into the compartment, took his seat at the window and stared out at the German Democratic Republic. Again the landscape had changed, this time dramatically. It seemed, apart from the ploughed fields, to be untouched. There were no houses, and the few roads he saw wound emptily past fields and woods and simply disappeared in the distance. The emptiness of the landscape reminded him of Africa. Occasionally a small Skoda car could be seen bouncing along the badly-kept roads, and as infrequently a far-away village. No houses, no petrol stations, no sign of any commerce was to be seen. He thought that this was how it could have looked in the eighteenth century. He heard Lilo turn over the pages of her notebook and then she said, "I see there is a gap."

"Oh? When was that?"

"After you left the camp at Bremerhaven. What happened then?"

Before he could answer, the door was pushed open by two East German Border Police. "*Passport, bitte*," one of them said. They were young men and the one who spoke had an air of toughness and authority. Spencer handed over his passport. The second policeman stood in the corridor looking casually over the compartment. The first man turned over the pages of the passport and then said something in German which Spencer did not catch. The policeman waited, took a step towards him and stretched out his hand and Spencer thought: *They know about the gun.*

He put up his own hand as though to ward off a blow. He heard Lilo say something, but the policeman's hand was in front of his face and he pushed it away.

"Mr Spencer," Lilo said. "He only wants you to take off your dark glasses."

He tried to smile. He took his glasses off. But the policeman was not to be mollified. He asked Spencer and Lilo to go into the corridor and the two began to search the compartment.

"I'm sorry," Spencer said, "I didn't realize . . ."

"You have made them angry."

The policeman told them to open their suitcases and they pulled the cushions out from the seats and felt under the seats and looked up on the racks and Spencer knew then that if they found the gun they'd take him off the train at Magdeburg. They searched for five minutes but they found nothing and he realized that it had been more of a reprisal than a search: they had not expected to find anything, just to disrupt. When they had gone he repacked his case and resumed his seat.

Lilo was looking at him oddly. He felt angry and embarrassed and when she said, "Can we go back to the . . ." he answered abruptly: "Do you mind . . . I'm a bit tired."

He sat watching the countryside unroll. At Magdeburg they stopped outside the station. Several East German local trains passed them. All the coaches were marked second class and the passengers sat on wooden benches. The station was crowded, so were the trains and the people looked dowdy in their simulated leather coats. They crossed the Elbe and went on towards Berlin.

"I'm sorry to trouble you, Mr Spencer," Lilo said, "but it will not be too long now and there are some questions I must ask."

"All right."

"When you left the camp at Bremerhaven the war was not yet over."

"It's very simple," he said, keeping as close to the truth as he could. "In Bremerhaven I'd been in a camp with older men. One of them had assaulted me. The commandant thought I'd be safer somewhere else. But there were no camps for sixteen-year-old boys. So I was sent to Berlin to be looked after by a family."

"You mean you were free?" she said, surprised.

"In a way."

"You, an Englishman, in the middle of Berlin in wartime?"

"I know it sounds crazy," he said, "but I wasn't the only one. There were others like me, also very young, too young for the camps."

He told her about the Gutmanns and Lange, editing everything but staying close enough to the facts.

"And these people have something to do with you now?" she said.

"I don't know," he said. "I haven't seen them since then."

"Can I ask then why you are going to Berlin?"

"I should have thought that was obvious."

"Forgive me?"

"Look at it from my point of view. Out of all the houses in Britain they chose mine. Why? Who do I know who could have caused this? The only people I know in Germany are the people I stayed with."

"What can they have to do with it?"

"Perhaps nothing. But then again they may. It's what I must find out."

"But the mother. Mrs——"

"Gutmann."

"She would be very old now. And so would the other gentleman. Lange."

"But not Bruno."

"Why don't you leave it to the police?"

"I have. They've achieved nothing."

"So what you are doing now——"

"What I'm doing now is finding out."

"But that is the question. After all these years *how* will you find out?"

"You'll help me."

She smiled at him uncertainly.

# *Berlin*

## PART III

His disorientation began at the Zoo Station. In his memory it was a building not unlike Waterloo Station in London, crowded with refugees and soldiers in field grey, with first aid posts and shelter signs and rubble. The train arrived at 6.30 and everything was much smaller than he recalled and much more modern. They took a taxi to his hotel in Kurfursten-strasse and when he looked at the map he realized that this was the way he and Bruno had walked on their visits to the house in Charlottenburg. Not a single thing brought back a memory except the ruin of the Gedächtniskirche. There was a sign which said Budapesterstrasse. This was where he had been beaten up. Now it could have been a street in any city in the world; nothing seemed the same. Everything was glass and concrete and trees; wide streets, modern buildings. In his mind it had been an old city, half-ruined, but now he realized that eventually it had been wholly ruined. Only when he saw all the new buildings did he realize the extent of the damage; for wherever a new building stood, an old one had been flattened.

At the hotel he said, "Come in for a drink."

"I'm sorry. I have things to do. Anyway, I must try and find out what happened to these people if I am to be of service to you."

"Don't take that too literally."

"From now on will be the best part for me," she said. "For my article. Especially if we find them. I have some contacts."

He paused, but she did not expand. "When will I see you?" he said.

"I will telephone you tomorrow."

He watched the taxi disappear and went up to his room. He poured himself a strong whisky from a litre he had bought in the duty-free shop on the ship and drank it quickly. He found

95

himself wondering where she was, what she was doing. She had told him she was divorced so she was not going home to a husband. But a lover? He ran a bath and lay in it sipping a second whisky. The picture he retained of her was when they had been walking up and down the station at Hanover: long, slender legs under a blue suede coat, red lips, very white teeth, black hair cut severely across her forehead. Then the image splintered as when a reflection in a pool is broken by a stone, and he saw Susan in the suede coat; Susan's long legs, Susan's dark hair, Susan's blue eyes. Rage suffused his body and he found he had squeezed the soap into a shapeless mass.

He dressed, put the gun in his coat pocket, covered it with his sheepskin, and went to an Italian restaurant almost directly opposite the hotel. He had a light meal and smoked a cigar with his coffee and thought of Lilo and her thin Dutch cheroots.

He had planned to wait until the following day before he began his inquiries, but it was too early to go to bed so, after standing outside the restaurant for a few moments in the biting wind he put up his sheepskin collar and began to walk east. He turned into Schillerstrasse in the direction of the Tiergarten. He recognized nothing, but under the bright light he could follow his route on a street map and soon he came to the great dark area of the park itself. The streets were empty and even the traffic was light. He turned right and made his way along Tiergartenstrasse. On his left side were the dark trees, on his right ... on his right there should have been streets and houses. Under the lights he could see streets neatly laid out; but there were no houses. It was like a housing project where the streets are laid down first while the lots are being sold. Then he realized he was in a kind of wasteland. These were bombed sites, like the ones he had seen in the fifties in the City of London. He could make out small piles of rubble, the bottom of a broken wall still with wallpaper clinging to it after all these years. Weeds had grown up, grass blew in the wind. He walked on and then he saw a metal sign which said Graf Speestrasse. Two houses still stood. One was almost completely cut off from the outside by shrubs and trees, the other seemed only habitable on the ground and basement floors; they stood there in derelict isolation, sole survivors of the bombing and shelling. He walked down the street a little way and stopped. Where the Gutmanns' house must have been there was only a weed-grown empty lot. He remembered Bruno saying of the bombers, "They cannot hit us". But they had.

He stepped off the kerb and into the weeds. His feet encountered loose bricks and pieces of plaster. He bent down and picked up a piece of wood and examined it under a street light. It could have come from anything, a joist, a rafter, a floorboard; he might once have walked on it. He shivered, but not with cold. In all the bright and shiny new city this was one place that still held its memories, one place that had not changed much.

He heard footsteps and looked up as a man in a check coat and cap passed him, going down towards the canal. They did not look at each other. Spencer stared at the weeds and the rubble. There was nothing to be found here.

Just then he heard a door open and close and he saw someone come up the basement steps of the partially habitable house. In the street lights he was casting a gigantic misshapen shadow. After a moment he saw that the distortion was caused because the person was carrying a heavy metal dustbin. There was a clang as the dustbin was put down ready for the morning collection and the figure turned to go down the steps.

"*Entschuldigen-Sie, bitte*," Spencer said.

The figure paused, turned, and he saw he was talking to a youth of about eighteen. The youth looked at him inquiringly, his feet already on the steps, his body poised for quick retreat. Phrases had been racing through Spencer's head, but none seemed to fit the occasion.

"*Bitte?*" the youth said.

"I'm sorry," Spencer said. "Excuse me. Do you speak English?"

"At school I am learning."

"Good. I have some questions."

"Ask, please."

"A long time ago, during the war, when I was about your age, I stayed in one of these houses."

"You lived here?"

"In the war. I was in the Merchant Navy and my ship was sunk." He saw the youth begin to look confused.

"You wish to know something?" He was dressed in a thin shirt and was beginning to shiver.

"The house was over there," Spencer said, pointing to a dark area of grass. "At least, I think so. A family named Gutmann."

"What is it you wish, please?"

"I am here on holiday. I wanted to find out what had happened to them."

"*Willi!*" a voice called from the house. "*Was macht du?*"

"*Ein moment.*" He turned to Spencer. "You wish to discover what happened to family Gutmann?"

"That's right."

"Come, please."

"Now?"

"Yes, please. You must ask my grandmother."

Spencer looked at his watch. "I could come back in the morning."

"My grandmother sleeps in the morning. Please do not worry. Other people are coming to ask such things."

"About the Gutmanns?"

"About many people."

"*Willi!*"

"*Ich komme!*" he shouted angrily. He beckoned Spencer to follow.

Spencer went down the basement steps at his heels. Willi stood aside and he stepped into the room. What he saw was like a physical blow. He was transported back in time to 1944, standing in the Gutmanns' sitting-room with Mrs Gutmann talking about the bombing. The big room was an almost exact replica of the Gutmanns' room, even to the baulks of timber along one wall that supported the ceiling and the floor above. There was the same heavy, ornate furniture, the same over-stuffed look where pieces seemed to vie with each other for space. In one corner was a large black wardrobe which reminded Spencer of the one in Bruno's bedroom, the one behind which he had kept his shoe-box containing the gold objects.

In front of him, seated at a dining-room table, or what looked like a dining-room table, for it was so heavily covered in newspapers he could not see its surface, sat an elderly woman in a wheel-chair. She was large and her flesh hung loosely on her; she had white hair and a high colouring. She was looking at Spencer in surprise.

"I found him outside," Willi said.

"Who is he?" They spoke rapidly in German and Spencer had difficulty in following.

"He has questions about the street."

"At this hour?"

"You said I must always tell you."

"Tell me, yes, but you can see I'm working." She indicated the newspapers in front of her. Spencer saw scissors and a pot of glue. He also noticed that piles of newspaper, some cut and some uncut, stood around the walls.

"I'm sorry," he said. "It's only a question or two."

"Ah, so, English," the old woman said. Then to Willi, "You didn't tell me he was English." She turned back to Spencer and said, labouring in the unfamiliar language, "I have your family." He raised his eyebrows and fixed a smile on his face. "I show you."

She turned her wheel-chair and propelled herself to the other side of the room where there were several shelves packed with large volumes. She pulled out one and brought it back to the table. The speed with which she moved made Spencer think this was a manoeuvre which she had carried out many times before. She placed the book on the table and opened it. "Come," she said. He found himself looking down at a wedding picture of Queen Elizabeth and the Duke of Edinburgh.

"Your family," the old woman said.

The entire scrapbook was given over to newspaper cuttings and pictures of the British Royal Family. She turned back and showed him the first picture in the book; it was of Princess Elizabeth leaning over a high verandah in what seemed a tropical country. Then he recognized it: it was one of the photographs taken at Treetops Hotel in Kenya in 1952. In the background he could see elephants drinking at a waterhole.

"She is there," the old woman said, tapping the picture, "when King of England dies." She turned the pages: there they all were, the Queen, the Duke, the Prince of Wales, Princess Anne, Buckingham Palace, Windsor, Balmoral, tartans, kilts, the corgis. Finally she closed the book and put it away.

"What does he want?" she asked Willi abruptly.

"It is about the street. The family Gutmann."

She looked quickly at Spencer and then away. "Tell him I'm tired," she said. But Willi's curiosity had been stimulated for he said, "My grandmother takes much interest in the street. She has lived since the war always in the same place. It is from the Russian guns she was paralysed in the legs. She is the only one left from the people who lived here. Sometimes persons like yourself come to ask questions to try and find relatives."

"Tell him to go away," she said. She had begun to cut and paste in a kind of fury.

Willi turned to her. "He used to live with the Gutmanns in the war."

She stopped her work and stared at Spencer. "I heard there was an Englishman there. A boy. But I didn't see him."

Willi translated. The old woman was clearly tired and would not speak English. "He wishes to know what happened to the family," Willi said.

She went on working furiously for a moment and then abruptly she threw down the scissors and paste and propelled herself back to the shelves and returned with another volume.

"This is the one of the people in the street," Willi said. "She knew most by their names. Many were killed in the bombings. But she has kept, how do you say it, trace . . ."

"Track."

"Track of some of them."

She opened the volume and Spencer could see short paragraphs cut from newspapers and an occasional picture. Her finger stabbed down on one page, and she began to speak.

**100**

"Fleischman. Professor. Doktor. J. Number 7. Died in Heidelberg in 1958. Wife had an affair with Herr Schalk who lived in number 42. They were divorced." She turned over a few pages and stabbed down again. "Family Neibuhr. Husband, wife, two daughters killed by the Russians in 1945. They lived at number 16." Another page, another stabbing finger. "Knopf. Number 23. He fell under the S-bahn in 1962. His wife had died from cancer. No one knows if he fell or threw himself." She turned several pages. "Here. Family Gutmann. Frau Gutmann had an affair with a lodger, Herr Lange. They disappeared in 1945."

She was about to close the book when Spencer said, "There are other cuttings there," and he moved to her side. He put his hand between the pages to keep it open. In the centre of one page was a picture from a glossy magazine of a beautiful fashion model. She had long dark hair, a wide mouth and high cheek bones, a Slavic face.

"Who is she?" he said.

She tried to close the book but he kept his hand there firmly.

"She's frightened," Willi said, and it was apparent that he was enjoying his grandmother's discomfiture. Spencer wondered if they lived together without other family; he wondered what hatreds lay just beneath the skin of their relationship.

The old woman turned and looked up at him and he could see the anxiety in her eyes.

Brutally he said, "Tell her I won't leave until she tells me."

She and Willi spoke rapidly and angrily to each other. Finally she broke off the conversation and sat with her head bowed.

Willi said, "She is the wife of the son. Her name is Gerda."

"The wife? Of Bruno?"

He nodded. "My grandmother is afraid of him. During the war, in the bombing, he came in and robbed her. He told her he would kill her if she spoke of it. She had always been afraid since then."

"Ask her to tell me about him now. I won't mention her."

The old woman shook her head. Then she said slowly in English, "They are divorced. Long ago. That is all I know."

She took Spencer's hand from the book, closed it, returned it to the shelves and sat facing the wall.

"You must go now," Willi said.

"I have some more questions."

"Not now."

"Tomorrow, then."

"Perhaps."

Spencer went down Graf Speestrasse in the direction of the canal. He wondered if the old woman knew more than she was saying. She had clearly been frightened. He would find out in the morning.

He stopped on Bendlers Bridge and stared down at the water. In the lights the trees were faintly reflected. It looked cold, but clear, very different from the last time he had stood there. Then he and Bruno had been coming home from an evening with Astley and Richards and they'd had to make a detour because some of the streets were closed from the bombing. They were being bombed almost every night of clear weather by Pathfinder Groups followed by thousand-bomber formations. The canal had been choked with rubble; the bush and grass had been neglected and had overgrown both banks.

They had stopped on the bridge and Bruno had said, "They say there are snakes here, pythons and God knows what, and crocodiles from the Zoo." The Zoo had been bombed the day before and dozens of animals were said to have escaped. "Never mind," Bruno said, putting an arm around his shoulders. "Not to worry."

"Lange says a tiger escaped and went into the Cafe Filz and ate some pastry and fell down dead."

"Another of his jokes."

Spencer moved out of his encircling arm. "He says the owners had a post mortem done to prove it wasn't their cakes."

"Very funny."

"He swears it's true."

"Listen, Johnnie, you must be careful of Lange. He's not one of us, you know. He's different. Always sneering and laughing up his sleeve." He had moved closer.

"He says Germany is going to lose the war," Spencer said. It was said to shock and Bruno took a step backwards. Spencer had expected anger but instead there was a look of sly acknowledgment in his eyes. "What does it matter for us? If the Allies win we will be all right. I have a British passport. I was brought over here by my mother. No one can say anything against me."

"What about me?"

"We'll stick together. Don't worry, Johnnie."

Mrs Gutmann was in the shelter under the house and Lange was at work when they got home. They went into the kitchen and Bruno said, "Look what I've got." From one of his coat pockets he pulled out a packet containing real coffee. It was the first coffee Spencer had seen since leaving England. Bruno made them each a mug and they sat down at the table to drink it.

"Astley and Richards are disgusting," Bruno said. "I hate the way they paw these women, don't you?"

"Yes." It was true, he did hate it. He hated being with them, hated it when they got drunk. He remembered what Lange had said about the Germans using people like Astley and Richards to boost civilian morale. Of late he had begun to understand what Lange had meant.

"Do you have a girlfriend back home?" Bruno looked up at him from under his eyebrows.

"No."

"Women are all right, but you cannot be friends with them. Not the sort of friendship that men have. There is a nobility in the friendship between two men that can never be between a man and a woman. Don't you think so, Johnnie?"

"I don't know."

"Look at us two. We are friends, isn't it?"

"Yes."

"And we are in danger. But we don't worry because we have each other. Whoever wins this war, it won't matter to us. In my school there was a big stained-glass window showing two soldiers in the first war. One of them had died trying to save the other. The words under the picture said, 'Greater love hath no man than he lay down his life for his friend.' That is what it is like between men, Johnnie."

They finished their coffee and Bruno said, "I'm going to sleep upstairs tonight. It's cloudy, there won't be a raid. Keep me company?"

"All right."

In the early hours of the morning Spencer woke. Someone was kneeling on his bed.

"What?" he said.

"It's me, Johnnie," Bruno whispered.

"What do you want?"

"Can't we be friends?"

"You're heavy."

"Give me your hand. Take it."

"No."

"Take it."

Spencer felt something hot and hard against his cheek. He fought as he had fought Campbell.

"It's all right, Johnnie. It's all right."

One of Spencer's arms was caught under the blankets and Bruno had the other. Bruno bent over his face. Spencer felt he was being suffocated. He shouted and pushed, as hard as he could. Bruno fell sideways to the floor and then the light was on and Lange was standing in the doorway. He stood there for some seconds taking in the scene and his mouth twisted downwards in disgust; then he switched out the light and closed the door.

The next morning at breakfast Bruno had described the incident as their "wrestling match" and had tried to laugh about it, but Lange had looked across the table at him and the disgust was still clear in his eyes. That was the last time Bruno referred to it. From then it was as though a wall had come between him and Spencer. Most days he left for the house in Charlottenburg or, at least, it was where he said he was going. He infrequently suggested now that Spencer should come with him. Once he took him to a barracks in Spandau where he said they were to learn to drill. But when they got there they found they were the only ones and after standing about on the icy

104

parade-ground for more than an hour Bruno said, "You'd better go back to the house," and left Spencer to get there as best he could. Later, Spencer was to learn that part of the Free Corps had been sent to help in Dresden, which had just been devastated by bombing.

It was a strange, dream-like time. Berlin was in chaos, every day saw major electricity failures, the trams were not running half the time, nor was the S-bahn; there were gas fires all over the city. The bombers droned in day after day to dump their loads. Thousands of refugees from the East lived in the bomb shelters, making it impossible for some Berliners to take shelter in a raid.

Bruno came and went from the house. He was employed by the Foreign Office and it was Spencer's impression that he was one of several young Germans whose job it was to look after members of the Free Corps. Often when Bruno came home he would go up to the bedroom and lock himself in. Spencer knew there were now two shoe boxes under the wardrobe but he was too scared to touch them

He spent much of his time in the villa. He watched the romance between Frau Gutmann and Lange bud and flower. It was clear that she was mothering him with those reserves of maternal feeling untapped by Bruno. She brought him little delicacies, bits of cheese, a slice or two of smoked sausage, a little coffee, when such things were almost as valuable as diamonds. Much of her day was spent standing in food queues, and since Lange worked shifts at the *Rundfunk* he and Spencer were thrown together. Lange told him at great length about Africa, about the great Namib Desert and the fringes of the Kalahari where the sands were a deep russet red. He also taught him chess. He was an excellent player and was far too good for Spencer but he played without his queen which made the games more interesting. For the rest, Spencer would walk around the shattered streets, careful now not to wear his uniform. It was on one of these walks that he met Annie. Her real name was Anna but after they had got to know each other she had asked him to call her Annie. She said it reminded her of her girlhood.

105

They met one afternoon in the Tiergarten. It was a beautiful winter's day, clear and sunny, and he had been walking with his eyes half closed against the brightness, hunched up in the sea coat he had managed to keep through his imprisonment, when he heard a voice saying, "Can you help me, please?" There was something about the inflection of the German words that made him stop and turn and he saw a large brunette in a fur coat pointing helplessly at one of the few surviving beech trees. "It is Ludi," she said, and again he heard the inflection. He looked up into the tree and saw a cat. It was a beautiful sealpoint Siamese and it sat hunched on one of the branches, unwilling to move either up or down. Then she spoke rapidly in German and he could not follow.

He said very slowly, "I cannot understand. Do you speak English?"

She looked at him in shocked amazement for a second and then burst out laughing. "English?" she said, and he heard the American accent. "I sure as hell do!"

So began for Spencer in those final months of the war when Germany was sliding quickly into ruin, one of the most intense periods of his life. He and Annie were two of a kind, strangers who found themselves alone in a foreign country in the midst of a war which had little or nothing to do with them. It was a friendship that started almost as a mother-son relationship, fulfilling both their needs, but then moved naturally into a second phase. Spencer became deeply in love with her: he at sixteen and a half, she at nearly forty. It was the first time he had ever been in love and while he never knew whether she really reciprocated his feelings, he was always to look back on his time with Annie with nostalgia and sadness.

But on that bright winter's day in the Tiergarten he had no idea that all this was yet to come. Annie stood with her hands on her ample hips, her fur coat blowing in the wind—to disclose a large Junoesque body—and said, "You're English, aren't you?"

"Yes."

"Where did you spring from? Are you a parachutist?"

"I'm here in a labour corps," he said, expressing for the first time the lie he was so often to use in the future.

Just then the cat gave a plaintive miaow and Annie said, "Ludi darling! Ludi . . . ?"

"I'll get him," Spencer said. He took off his coat and shinned up the tree and managed to get onto the branch where the cat lay. But Ludi had never seen him before and was not about to be handled. Each time he reached out the cat hissed and spat at him and when his hands finally came close enough it lashed out, raking the back of his right hand with razor-sharp claws. After a tussle in which both hands were scratched he managed to muffle it up inside his jersey and bring it down.

Annie had been standing under the tree laughing at his ineffectual efforts but her laughter turned to sympathetic concern and she insisted he come back to her apartment where she could bathe the scratches in antiseptic. She lived on the top floor of a six storey building past the Potsdamerplatz. From her window she could look south-west over Berlin. The apartment consisted of a bedroom containing a large double bed, a bathroom which led off it, and a small sitting-room/dining-room. The furniture was different from that which he had grown used to in Frau Gutmann's house; Annie's was all chrome tubing and canvas and she was later to tell him of the Bauhaus school of design.

She gave him tea without sugar or milk or lemon but he did not mind; he would have drunk sewer water just to be with her in the apartment. He had never seen anything like it. It was elegant and, although small, the furniture seemed to make it spacious. In Frau Gutmann's house the rooms were crammed with furniture, here there were few pieces and the apartment seemed to have more space than the house.

He watched her move about the room. She was a big woman. Her face was large, with good strong bones and her dark hair was worn in a roll under a white turban. While he was with her Spencer forgot the war, forgot his anomalous and dangerous position, in fact he forgot everything except being in this quiet elegant place with a woman who seemed to be interested in him.

107

She had all the directness of her countrymen, and it was something he had never encountered before. "Tell me about yourself," she said simply, once they had started their tea. If it had been anyone else he would have felt disconcerted but there was such warmth in Annie, such interest, amusement and sympathy, that he found himself telling her about his home in Bromley and about his parents and about running away to sea, everything, in fact, except what had happened to him in the camp and why he was in Berlin. It was the beginning of the secretive part of his personality.

Darkness was falling when he left. It was a moment he had been putting off, the time when he would have to face the real world again and leave the cosy warmth of her flat. But she said, "Come again, I haven't talked English like this for years". And he did come again. He came the following day and the day after that and the one after that until it became almost a set routine that in the afternoons he went to Annie's apartment for tea. Sometimes she would not be there and would leave a note for him on the door and he would feel devastated as he turned back into the bomb-torn streets. But mostly his knock would be answered and she would stand in the doorway and say "Hi", and for at least the next hour or two he would be in a kind of heaven. It never occurred to him that her apartment might be bombed; it was inviolate, enchanted.

After a few visits she began to talk to him about her life. She had been born in Fredericksburg in the hill country of Texas and still had a slight "y'all" accent. He learned that the small town had been founded by a group of German immigrants in the nineteenth century and had retained its German character even to the signs in the windows which said "English spoken here". Everything was German, from the cooking and baking to the style of dress, to the weekly newspapers. And he was reminded, as she spoke, of the part of the world where Lange had come from. They sounded similar.

By the time she was in her late teens she had developed an interest in singing. She was the soloist at the local Lutheran church and in her last years at high school had travelled all over Texas singing with the Fredericksburg choir. She studied first with a voice teacher in San Antonio, and from there she had gone to New York. In the early thirties her parents, who thought of Hitler as the new Messiah, decided to send her to the conservatorium in Berlin.

"I should have done it earlier," she said. "I was in my twenties before I came to Germany and that's too late. But I was having such a darn good time at home."

It transpired that her voice was not as good as had been thought and so when she met Herr Beckmann, who was twenty years older than she, but who owned a successful printing works, a house in Grunewald and a cottage in the mountains and who professed to be deeply in love with her, she decided to give up her training and marry him. "I wasn't getting any younger."

They had had no children, which was perhaps fortunate, because when Herr Beckmann was killed in a train crash in 1943 she discovered that the printing works was deeply in debt. After everything was sold, including the two houses, there was just enough left over to give her a small annual income. When she spoke about her husband it was in a remote way as though he had been a friend in the forgotten past, but even so Spencer felt a stab of jealousy. Once he said, "Did you love him?"

"In a way."

"There's only one way," he said fiercely.

"When you grow up you'll find that there are many ways."

It was in the third week of their relationship that they went to bed together and Spencer began the last stage of growing up.

Later, whenever he thought about it he found it difficult to recall exactly how it had happened. It had started innocently enough. She had taken to giving him a kiss on the cheek when he arrived for his tea each day. It was simply an affectionate peck. She would open the door, say, "Hi, how are you?" and kiss him—all in the same action. But on this particular day he arrived as one of her neighbours was leaving, an elderly man who lived on the floor below and who had come to borrow a pillow. After Spencer had shaken his hand and the old man had thanked Annie and by the time they were inside the flat, the pattern had been broken. She closed the door behind her and greeted him for a second time and took his face in her hands and would have kissed him on the forehead, but in that second, without giving it even a moment's thought, he moved his head so that their lips met and he put his arms up to her shoulders.

He had never had a girlfriend; the position of his father had militated against that as it did against so many other things. His memory of women dated from the time, when he was about nine years old and he and a friend and the friend's sister had played postman's knock and Spencer and the sister had spent most of a wet afternoon under an eiderdown kissing as passionately as their prim and closed lips would allow. He had also felt the child's budding breasts and had left feeling slightly dazed by so unexpected a launching into Life.

And now, again, his primly closed lips pressed chastely on Annie's. She gave a startled chuckle and held him at arm's length for a moment as she looked at him. And then she said, and he hardly recognized her voice. it had grown so husky, "You're a very beautiful young man and it's time you learned for your own sake." She kissed him in an entirely new way, forcing his lips open until they tasted each other and he felt her body shudder.

"I think we'd better postpone our tea," she said.

In the days that followed he explored her body as a traveller might explore a golden land which he had seen in his dreams but had never thought to reach. She was a woman running to fat with big breasts, buttocks and thighs, but Spencer, now in the grip of erotic love, did not see the collapsing flesh. Instead he saw her as Titian might have seen his models: an amplitude of curves and planes, of convex surfaces and concave hollows, of dark shadowy places. Once she had taught him to make love he was voracious.

After that first remark she never used the word "young" again. She never said, "I'm old enough to be your mother," or "I could have had a son your age". She treated him as an equal both in years, in emotion and in sexual need. She had had casual affairs after the death of Herr Beckmann, but most with men who went off to the Front and never came back.

110

Now she had someone of her own, yet she never considered it as even semi-permanent. She took each day by itself, never looking into the future and never into the past. Often, as the spring days began to lengthen, they would make love and then walk in the Tiergarten among the bombed and splintered trees and she would take Ludi on a lead with a little silver collar round his neck and Spencer would make believe they were married. He yearned to talk of the future as all young men do; he was frightened to think of the past and the present was only a stepping-stone. But even he realized that as Berlin burned to death the future was too ominous even to contemplate.

It was in these circumstances one afternoon, lying in her big double bed under every blanket in the flat because there was no heating, that she had begun to ask him questions about the recent past, probing more deeply than she had before, sensing that there was something there that he had not told her. Then, for the first and only time in his life, Spencer told another human being the truth about why he was in Berlin.

She listened, cuddling up at his back, so that they lay like two S's together, and he could feel her big warm breasts against his skin. He had kept lying the way he was, fearing what she might think or say, fearing to see a change in her eyes, but when he'd finished she turned him over and held him in her arms. "Try not to worry about it," she said and there was no hint of condemnation in her voice, rather the opposite, for she was quickly sympathetic in all things. "We'll figure something out."

He always remembered that moment; it was the one time he had felt totally secure; he was never to feel that way again.

\*       \*       \*

"My God," Spencer said, looking down at his plate, "I'll never get through this."

He and Lilo were lunching at a Balkan restaurant near the Wittenbergplatz. He had ordered the *hausplatte*, thinking that it would be a kind of *plat du jour*, and now he looked in disbelief at the large rectangular plate that had been placed in front of him. It was heaped with pieces of grilled meat

111

and sausages, mounds of rice, Liptauer cheese and several salads.

"You should have warned me," he said.

"I thought you knew."

She was having an omelette, but even that was the size of a large Spanish tortilla. She smiled at him and again he noticed the white even teeth against the red of her lips and he felt an unexpected flicker of excitement, accompanied almost immediately by a spurt of guilt. He ate in silence.

He had spent a frustrating morning. He had gone back to the house in Graf Speestrasse but no one had answered his knocking. He had circled the house, walking among the rubble but had been unable to see inside. He had knocked and shouted until a passerby had looked at him suspiciously and he knew that if he kept it up someone would call the police. What made it worse was that he *knew*, because there was no way of getting her wheel-chair up the steps, that the old woman was in the room. He had picked up a cab and gone to the Europa Centre and had a cup of coffee, watching two old couples skate round the ice-rink. Perhaps Willi only came back in the evenings, perhaps that was the time to return.

Where else could he start his search? The Gutmanns' house, his one real link, had simply been wiped out as writing is wiped from a blackboard. He supposed there must be records of bombed families and what had happened to them. This was where Lilo Essenbach came in. In the meantime he had one lead: Bruno's ex-wife. But what was her name? Gutmann? He had already looked in the telephone directory and there was no Gerda Gutmann or Bruno Gutmann, for that matter. No, the old woman would have to give up her secret. He would wait until dark.

At the hotel there was a message for him. Lilo was waiting at a bar-restaurant nearby. Would he join her there?

"Eat," she said. "You'll enjoy it."

He could not recognize the pieces of meat. "That's pork fillet," she said, pointing. "And lamb. And beef. That is a piece of veal. Those are *cevapcicis*—spiced sausages." They ate in silence and he watched her. She was hungry and ate with

112

relish. He ate as much as he could, but left half. They had coffee and he smoked one of her cheroots.

"Well?" he said.

"It is not easy. But not impossible. I used to work for *Bild*. I still have some old contacts in the Ministries."

"I'll show you where the house was, if you like."

"First, I must go to the toilet."

She went into the back of the restaurant. He smoked the last of his cheroot. He was sitting facing the road and he noticed that it was beginning to snow. Just then a dark blue furniture van came to a stop outside the window, blocking his view of the street. But it gave him another view; it acted as a mirror and he was able to see himself as well as the restaurant behind his back. There was a passage leading away to the kitchens and, he assumed, the lavatories. And then he saw Lilo. She was at the end of the bar with her back to him and she was using the telephone on the wall. She spoke hurriedly, replaced the receiver, walked into the darkened passage and a moment later re-entered the room, smoothing down her coat.

"Shall we go?" she said.

She drove an Opel Manta that had seen better days and took him back the way he had walked the night before. In the daylight the dereliction did not look so bad. The streets were clean, the bomb sites neat. There was no sign of life in the old woman's house, but again he had the feeling of being watched.

"This is where the house used to be," he said.

"They are going to redevelop the whole area."

A blue Beetle pulled up in the wasteland by the canal. A man and a woman in the front began to kiss passionately. "Lunch-time lovers," Spencer said.

She laughed uncertainly. "They must go somewhere."

"There was another house I used to visit. In Charlottenburg. Maybe it's still there."

"Do you know the address?"

"No. It was near water."

She looked mystified.

"The road went over a sort of lake. Not a very big one. Rather pretty."

She took out a street map and they looked at it together. His head was close to her hair and he smelled its fragrance; for a moment he hated her.

"It must be the Lietzensee Park."

They drove along Kantstrasse until they came to the park. In the grey afternoon light the water was like an engraving.

"Is that it?" she asked.

"It could be. It looks different."

They turned right and drove slowly up and down the streets of terraced housing. Some houses were new, some had survived the war and still bore the scars of shrapnel and bullets. On others the holes had been filled with cement, which gave them a slightly patchwork look.

"Do you recognize anything?"

"It was in a street like this."

"What did you do in this house?"

"As far as I can remember we had endless talks about National Socialism and what would happen when National Socialism ruled the world."

"You never told me of this."

"No."

"You never told me what you did in Berlin."

"I was in a sort of labour corps. Cleaning the rubble off the streets after the bombing."

"And you came here in the evening to talk about National Socialism? At sixteen?"

"I didn't talk about it. I listened."

"This is the part I do not understand."

"First of all, remember that a lot of strange things happened at that time. Remember Dresden had been bombed. Berlin had even more refugees than before. The whole city was collapsing."

"Go on."

There was no escape from it now. "There was an organization called the Free Corps. The British Free Corps. Have you heard of it?"

"No."

He explained as best he could but even so he could see

114

she hardly understood. "But what did you have to do with them?"

"Bruno took me along. He thought I'd like to meet some Englishmen."

He remembered one evening with great clarity. It was very near the end. Astley and Richards were living in an alcoholic daze. The Russians were a hundred kilometres from the city and no one had time to worry about a few English traitors. But orders had been given for the men to be paid and with Teutonic thoroughness these orders were carried out, even in the last desperate days. They all had money for drink and women; there was *Götterdämmerung* in the air. Bruno was in a constant state of nervous excitement. Since the night he had come to Spencer's bed they had been distant. So when one night Bruno said that they would go and see Astley and Richards he had felt surprised and somewhat nervous.

They had sat in the downstairs room of the Charlottenburg house drinking cheap wine. There were three girls this time and amid winks and nudges and changings of place Spencer found himself sitting next to one of them. And then, clearly according to some prearranged plan, they had grabbed him and held him on the floor and pulled his trousers down. One of the girls painted his genitals with blue ink. He fought and there were tears in his eyes and Astley had the grace to look embarrassed.

"It's just initiation, old chap," he said thickly.

Then they went out drinking and left him alone with one of the girls.

"You don't have to do anything," she said indifferently. She pulled out some knitting and began to work at it. "For my friend," she said. "To keep him warm."

Spencer left before the others returned. It took him two days to get rid of the stain, two days before he could return to Annie.

Lilo spent another half hour driving him up and down the streets of Charlottenburg, but he could not place the house. She took him back to the hotel and said, "I have calls to make. I will telephone you later."

He watched her drive down Kurfurstenstrasse in the direction of the centre of town, then turned away to enter the hotel. As he did so his eye caught another car. It passed the hotel, turned right and went out of sight. It was a blue Beetle and he was sure it contained the lunchtime lovers he had seen earlier.

Thoughtfully, he crossed the lobby towards the elevators. A figure rose from a chair to his right and came towards him.

"May I speak with you, please?"

He turned and saw it was Willi. He was dressed in a suit and looked older and more self-possessed than he had the night before.

Spencer pointed to the far corner of the lounge. "What about over there? Would you like something to drink?"

"Coffee, perhaps."

He ordered two coffees and said, "How did you know I was here?"

"I followed you."

"When?"

"Last night."

"Why?"

Willi shrugged. "I thought we must do business some time."

"Aah," Spencer said. "I see." He looked at him carefully for the first time. The night before he had briefly absorbed him as a tall, reasonably good-looking, fair-skinned, fair-haired young man. Now on closer examination he saw that the eyes were close together and there was a pubescent moustache on his upper lip. The combination gave him a foxy look.

The coffee arrived and Spencer poured it. When the waiter was out of earshot he said, "Tell me what business you think we have to transact."

Willi sipped his coffee then said, "First please let me explain something. The . . . business—"

"Let's not call it business. Let's call it by its real name: money."

Willi shifted uneasily. "All right. If you wish it."

"Now you can explain."

"My parents died a long time ago. I have lived with my grandmother. She looked after me. Now she grows old and I must look after her."

116

"That's the way it goes."

"I have nearly nineteen years, my grandmother has more than seventy. But she is strong. Paralysed in the legs, yes, but she is strong in the body. You see?"

Spencer was not totally unfamiliar with the situation and he could find it in himself to sympathize with the boy. "What are you proposing to do about it?"

"That is why I need money. There is a place for such people. Like apartments more than a hospital. You have a room and a bathroom and kitchen. There are nurses and doctors to look after you. But you must buy the apartment and it is very expensive. I have some money from my parents but I must have more."

"What about the house? The site alone must be worth a lot."

"Many times there have been people wishing to buy but she will not sell. She wishes to die in this house."

"So how will you get her to your hos—the apartment."

"There are ways," Willie said, and Spencer had a picture of ambulances and strait-jackets. But maybe it wasn't like that; maybe things were ordered differently these days.

"You say you want to do business, but that's a trade; it depends what you have to trade."

"You are looking for someone."

"Bruno Gutmann."

"I can give you the name of the lady in the picture."

"His ex-wife?"

"That is correct."

"How much?"

He had expected Willi to look embarrassed but the foxy face did not change. "Two thousand marks."

"That's ridiculous."

"How much will you pay?" For the first time there was a touch of nervousness, a hint that he really was only eighteen.

"A thousand."

Willi nodded. "All right."

He handed Spencer a piece of paper on which was written the name 'Gerda Riesenfeld'.

117

"Is that all? What about the address?"

Willi smiled. "That will be extra."

"How much extra?"

"Two thousand marks."

Spencer watched him leave the hotel. Was this how Bruno had started? Selling information? On an impulse he crossed to the public telephone and pulled out the directory. He paged over until he came to R. There it was: Riesenfeld, Gerda. He compared the address in Grunewald with the one Willi had sold him. They were identical. Perhaps this was all Willi had done for his two thousand marks, just opened the telephone book. He'd go far, Spencer thought.

*     *     *

It was dark when the taxi drew up at the house in Grunewald. Spencer asked the driver to wait and went up the steps. It was a large house which had been split up into several apartments and he found Gerda Riesenfeld's name above a bell at the side of the house. He rang and as he did so he noticed that the door was partially open.

"Is that you, Heinz?" a woman's voice called in German. "I've been waiting."

Spencer opened his mouth to explain and thought how ridiculous it would sound shouting in English, so he pushed the door and went into a carpeted hall.

"Hurry!" the woman shouted.

He looked up and saw her standing at the bannisters near the top of the stairs. The light was on above her and he could see her plainly while he himself remained in semi-darkness. She was in her late forties or early fifties and he knew, from the picture in the album, that once she had been beautiful. Now she was so thin she looked as though she had been mummified. The skin was stretched tight over her bones and her nose had hooked downwards. Her hair was jet black, she wore a black roll-neck sweater and black slacks and her face was dead white, as though she had covered it with rice powder.

Spencer mounted the stairs towards her. She was scratching at her left forearm.

118

"You are not Heinz," she said in German as he came up the stairs into the light. "Who are you? What do you want?"

"I'm sorry. I didn't mean to frighten you. I wanted to see Fraulein Riesenfeld."

"You cannot walk into someone's house." She, too, spoke in English, heavily accented but otherwise fluent.

"The door was open."

"That does not give you permission."

While she spoke she looked past him to the open front door.

"Forgive me. I didn't mean to trespass. Are you Fraulein Riesenfeld?"

She yawned and shivered slightly. "I cannot see you now."

"It won't take long."

He was standing half way up the staircase and she was above him. Suddenly she raised her arms and screeched at him and he was reminded of a large black bird about to take flight. "Can't you hear? Have you no ears? I cannot see you! I do not wish to speak with you!"

"Five minutes. I've come a long way. All the way from England. It's about Bruno."

"Bruno?" She looked at him owlishly.

"Bruno Gutmann. Perhaps you knew him under another name. I'm talking about your former husband."

She went quite still. "What do you know of Bruno?"

"That is what I want to ask you. But not here, shouting at each other on the staircase."

She scratched at her arm again. "You have come from England to talk about Bruno? Is he dead? Has he left me his money?" She gave a nervous, rasping laugh.

She walked through a doorway to her left. Spencer went up the stairs and followed her. It was a small sitting-room. An attempt had been made to furnish it elegantly. There were one or two good antique chairs and a low coffee table. In one corner was a divan with a rug thrown back and a pillow still bearing the indentation of a head. The room was squalid: coffee cups were scattered about on every available flat surface. Cigarettes had been stubbed out in the ashtrays and when these had filled up, in the stale fluid in the cups. Magazines were scattered about. There were newspapers on the floor. Part of a half-eaten sandwich had been thrown on the carpet. The room had not been dusted for weeks and the heavy curtains looked as though they were permanently drawn.

She waved vaguely at the mess. "The maid did not come today." She lit a cigarette and stood in the middle of the room scratching her elbow. Now, closer to her, Spencer could see that her skin had a slight blue tinge.

"I give you two minutes," she said.

"It's quite simple. I'm looking for Bruno."

Again she gave that harsh rasping laugh, the air hissing out between her teeth, sending jets of smoke into the room. "You are looking for Bruno. That is good. Why?"

"It's a long story and you said only two minutes."

"Make it short."

"I was in Berlin at the end of the war. I knew Bruno then. And his mother. I thought I'd like to make contact again. Find out what's happened in these years."

"You wish me to believe that? You come to my house in the night to ask questions. You have my address, why do you not use the telephone?" He had considered the telephone, but rejected it. It was too easy to refuse information on the telephone.

He caught a slight sound in the hall outside. She heard it, too. She had been listening with her whole body like some feeding antelope that senses danger in the nearby bush.

"It is someone I must see. Please wait here."

She went out and closed the door. Spencer could hear a man's voice. It sounded angry. Then he heard the woman's. It started off on a pleading note and rose almost to a point of hysteria. They seemed to argue for some minutes then the front door slammed and he heard her feet on the staircase. She closed the door of a room nearby and there was silence for a while. Spencer stood uneasily, waiting. He picked up a magazine. It was the American edition of *Harper's Bazaar*. He looked more closely at the cover. The picture was of Fraulein Riesenfeld modelling a fur coat. The date was Christmas, 1965. He picked up one or two magazines. There was a *Vogue* also dating from 1965 and a *Marie Claire* from 1966. She was on the covers of both.

He was still holding one when she came back. She had a vacant look on her face, as though she was drowsy from a long sleep. She walked past him and lit another cigarette. "I was beautiful, no?"

"Very."

"Bruno thought so too. But for him I was beautiful like Ming. Do not touch, eh? Only young boys."

"Yes, I know."

"You, too?"

"No, not me."

She lay down on the divan and pulled the blanket up over her legs. "So," she said. "You want to know where Bruno is." Her voice was thick and warm.

"Yes."

She smiled at him. "Everybody wants to know where Bruno is. Even the police."

She closed her eyes. He knew that she'd had her fix and that she was going to sleep and there was nothing he or anyone else could do about it. She was snoring by the time he left.

He was in his hotel room having a whisky when Lilo phoned. "You were not asleep?"

"No."

"I telephoned before."

"I went for a walk." He thought her voice sounded suspicious.

"There is some news. I think I have found Lange."

"Lange!"

"Yes, it is good, not so?"

"Where are you? Can we meet?"

"It is late."

"Nonsense."

She hesitated, then said, "All right. The restaurant where we had lunch."

It was cold and there were few people about. There was only one table occupied in the restaurant and the bar was empty. A waitress stood at the mouth of the corridor that led to the kitchens, obviously waiting for the last diners to finish so they could close. Spencer sat on a bar stool and ordered schnapps and a packet of Villigers. The taste of schnapps *was* Berlin to him. The first time he had ever had it had been at the Charlottenburg house. He kept turning towards the street until he realized there was a mirror above the bar in which he could watch the door. It reminded him of the mirror which the furniture van had formed when they had been lunching there, and how he had seen Lilo at the telephone. Had she lied then? Not necessarily. She had decided to make a telephone call, that was all. But if that was all, why had she pretended to go to the lavatory?

There was a movement in the mirror and he watched the door open and saw her come in with that long-legged, swinging stride. He found himself unfamiliarly disturbed. They took their drinks to a booth under the frowning gaze of the waitress and Lilo sipped hers nervously. It was apparent that she was in a highly excited state.

"I never thought you'd find Lange," he said. "I don't know why. It just never occurred to me. You've done well."

"Yes."

"Where is he? How do I get in touch with him?"

"Wait. There are problems."

He offered her one of his cigars but she took out her own packet and lit one. "We're lucky," she said.

"How is that?"

"I mean, to have found him. At first I had no luck. In each of our administrative districts during the war there was a *Vermissten-Nachweis*. You would call it a Bureau of Missing Persons. The names were given by the relatives or neighbours. But there was no Gutmann or Lange in that area. So I went to look at the records of the *Vermissten-Nachweis Zentrale* where there is an *Abteilung Tote*—a Dead Person's Department."

She went on to describe the operation of the various official bodies that had tried to keep records in a Berlin where everything was being ripped to pieces by bombs and shells: the *Sicherheits und Hilfsdienst*, the Repair Service that recovered the bodies. She told him how the dead were lined up on the pavements; how all valuables, including jewellery, papers, letters and rings were placed in separate envelopes on which was written the place, the date of discovery, the body's sex and, if known, the person's name.

"And the names weren't there?"

"That's right."

"But you found Lange. Where the hell is he? I thought he'd be dead by now."

"You're going too fast."

He realized she was going to tell it in her own way. "I'm sorry. Go on."

"I was looking for some record of one of them. You know Berlin was, how do you say it, 'chaos' . . ."

"Chaotic."

". . . chaotic at the end of the war. I think maybe it is easier to trace dead people. There are lists, names. But living people who do not have houses any more, that is more difficult."

"So . . ."

"So I remembered that you said Lange worked for the *Rundfunk*. I have a contact there. They still have all the files of their employees. Lange lives now in the East Zone."

He felt some of the excitement drain away. "You mean in East Germany?"

"No, here in the city, but in the east, beyond the Wall."

"Beyond the Wall!" They sat looking at each other and then he said, "Have another?"

She shook her head. "Come, let us go. They want to close."

The other diners had left and the waitress was hovering.

They stood outside on the pavement. "The hotel is just around the corner," he said. "Let me give you a drink there."

"Thank you."

But the lounge was dark so they went up to his room and he gave her a whisky in one of the tooth glasses.

"How do I get to him?" he said.

She was sitting on the one comfortable chair in the room and he stood at the window looking out at the lights. Suddenly a flash of memory came to him of his own study in Hampstead where he so often looked down on the lights of London.

"There is a possibility that something can be done. I have

**123**

made some telephone calls. I have relatives in the East Zone, it is not so difficult. People go backwards and forwards all the time."

"So you can get messages through?"

"Sometimes. Tomorrow you must take the afternoon tour of East Berlin. The buses leave from the top of the Kurfurstendamm. If anything can be done I will let you know. If not, then at least you will see East Berlin." She finished her whisky. "I must leave now."

"Stay with me."

"I cannot."

"It would mean a lot." Even as he said it a feeling of self-disgust swept over him.

She smiled, a rather sad and pensive smile, and touched him briefly on the cheek with her hand. "Thank you," she said, then she picked up her coat and left.

*     *     *

"Schmidt City Tours" said the legend on the bus that stood at the top of the Kurfurstendamm. It was a single-decker blue bus with a perspex roof tinted amber. Spencer stood on the pavement near it, waiting until almost the last minute, searching the lunchtime crowds for Lilo. A grey-haired man sat in the front of the bus with a sheaf of papers on his lap and a book of tickets. As each group of tourists climbed aboard he flashed them a smile, all teeth, and took their money in exchange for a ticket. They were due to depart at one-thirty. At twenty-nine minutes past, Spencer stepped aboard.

"Last but not least," the guide said, smiling. He checked Spencer's ticket and visa which the hotel had arranged for him that morning, then closed the door and stood up.

"My name is Harry," he said, in an American-German accent. "I would like to be your guide on this afternoon's tour, but it is impossible. You will be given a guide at the border. So I must just say one or two things. Please have your passports ready. Please do not try to leave the bus. Please do not try to change money in the East Zone. I tell you these things for your own sake. Now this is your driver," he indicated the man already at the wheel, "and I leave you to enjoy your tour." He got off, the bus started and within five minutes they had left the modern, glittering buildings behind and had reached a collection of dreary streets with old grey apartment blocks. Spencer saw for the first time what the division of the city meant. Along one street, every building had its windows blocked with concrete. Down the middle, zig-zagging away into the distance, was the Wall itself. On the West German side it was painted a light grey, but on the East side, as though to ameliorate its function, it was decorated in bright patterns.

The bus stopped at Checkpoint Charlie, which looked like a small city car park surrounded by wire and which contained two wooden huts from which the East German border guards operated. The driver switched off the engine and they sat and waited. Occasionally one of the guards came out of the hut, locked the door behind him and entered one of the other three tour buses waiting in the car park. Everything was done in slow motion. Passports were collected, papers checked. At last one of the buses moved off through the checkpoint and then the police turned their attention to the next. Spencer's bus was less than half full, mainly, it seemed, of American families from the Rhine Army bases.

Up to the last moment, he had expected a message. He had felt sure Lilo would meet him at the bus, but she had not. What was it she had said? "If anything can be done I will let you know; if not, then at least you will see East Berlin." Was that all he was achieving, a tour of the city? He watched the police dealing with the other buses. It took fifteen or twenty minutes to clear each of them and it was apparent that this was part of the East German policy, to make things as unpleasant as possible. Another bus left; now there was only one to go before it was their turn.

He had always thought that Checkpoint Charlie must be a romantic place. There was nothing romantic about these dingy surroundings. The door of the bus opened and a woman police officer entered. She was young and plain and wore a severe expression. She came down the middle aisle collecting passports. She took his, opened it, checked it against the information

125

on her list and then said something to him. This time he reached up and took his own dark glasses off. She nodded and gave him back his passport. She checked everyone. But then, instead of releasing the bus as she had the previous three she spent some seconds looking at the typed list in her hand, and collected all the passports. She went back to the hut, closed the door, and they were waiting again. Some of the Americans began to complain about the delay. A blonde woman asked the driver if he could switch on the engine and start the heating, for it was cold in the bus. He shrugged and said no, that the East German police would not like it.

"Where the hell do they get off, keeping us waiting like this?" the blonde woman said. She was middle-aged and had two teenage children with her. She spoke in Spencer's general direction but he looked away, staring at the grey streets.

In spite of the cold he felt himself begin to sweat. What was wrong, why were they being held up? Checkpoint Charlie was an urban no-man's-land and his passport had been taken away. He felt naked and somewhat afraid. Why hadn't they held up the other buses?

His thoughts came back to Lilo. There were things about her behaviour that left question marks. The telephone in the restaurant, for instance. And why had she never given him a telephone number or an address where he could contact her? It was always she who was going to ring him. And anyone could pretend to be a journalist, especially a free-lance.

He thought of the camera. An East German Praktica. Why wasn't she using one of a dozen West German or Japanese cameras that were as good or better? He remembered her on the train. She had started to interview him without even taking a note-book out. He had had to remind her. And then she had stopped taking notes. He remembered vividly something she had said: "I've checked my notes and there's a gap." The gap, of course, was after he had left Bremerhaven. But she hadn't taken notes about that part of his story. She had become so interested her pen had stopped. If she wasn't who she said she was, then who was she? He rubbed at the inside of the perspex roof that was now becoming covered by condensation

126

and saw his own face, drawn and grey like the streets outside; his eyes wide and staring. Why hadn't she sent him a message? There were questions everywhere. Unless she was on *their* side. What if they had been watching Spencer for weeks? What if they *wanted* him to come to East Berlin—oh, Jesus, he thought, what if Bruno was in East Berlin? What if she had lied about Lange?

The door of the bus opened and the policewoman was back, this time with an assistant, a man whose uniform looked too big for him and who had a pinched, unpleasant bureaucrat's face.

"Please, everybody come out," the policewoman said.

Again there were mutterings from the Americans, but they all clambered out into the car park in the bitter wind. The man went into the bus and looked under the seats and then made the driver open the spare wheel compartment under the body of the bus.

The blonde woman said, "My God, they can't be serious, can they?"

"They're serious, all right," Spencer said.

"But who would want to be smuggled *into* East Berlin?"

The policewoman made them line up in single file and as she called each person's name he had to step forward to be checked against her list before receiving back his passport. One after another they went up to be inspected, then they climbed back into the bus. When the last one came aboard the policewoman made a series of ticks on her documents and then held her hand up to the bus-driver to indicate that they were free to go. No one told them why this had happened, and after passing through the checkpoint they picked up their tour guide. She was a fair-haired woman in her fifties wearing a black plastic jacket. Her sallow face had an exhausted look, but she did her best to promote an atmosphere of cheerfulness in the bus.

They went along Friedrichstrasse and came almost immediately to Unter den Linden. She pointed out the Brandenburg Gate on their left and then they swung right on the huge boulevard. The differences Spencer had noted in the country-side between West and East Germany were sharpened and heightened here. West Berlin's polychromatic streets with their hoardings and flashing neon gave way to empty vistas, long, long streets with no one in them, only the occasional People's Car, a Wartburg or a Skoda. He could see places on old buildings where once there had been advertisements or shop names. The lettering had been ripped off but had left shadowy impressions on the concrete. Their guide talked without ceasing. She pointed out the Soviet Embassy, itself the size of a city block, the opera house, Humboldt University and, dominating every view, the TV tower. They passed a large open space and she said, "This is Marx-Engelsplatz. Here once stood the old Imperial Palace which was damaged during the war. We have no need for palaces in the Democratic Republic so we pulled it down. Now we come to our first halt".

They drove through a series of smaller streets until they stopped outside a building where all the shrapnel marks had been cut out and the squares filled with matching concrete. "This is the most famous museum in all Germany," she said. "The Pergamon Museum. We go in now for fifteen minutes." They trooped off the bus. The interior of the museum was cold and poorly lit; the grey afternoon light seeped through the long windows.

Spencer tried to keep in the middle of the group. It would make things more difficult for anyone to approach him. He had given up by now the thought that a message would reach him, instead he was afraid that something, he didn't know what—kidnap, assassination, something—might happen to him.

"This was once the main street of Pergamum," the guide said as they came into a hall lined with friezes. "They are the largest classical architectural structures in any museum of the world." They saw the Pergamon Altar and the Ishtar Gate and rooms full of Islamic and Middle Eastern art, then the guide said, "The fifteen minutes have finished. We must come to the bus now."

Their next stop was the Russian Memorial in Treptow. "Here we can get out . . ." she looked at her watch, ". . . for ten minutes. We must be back in the bus in ten minutes." The memorial was built on a vast scale, with an avenue about a hundred metres long leading up to the huge figure of a Russian soldier. Bas-reliefs showed episodes from World War II. "These have been made from the marble from the Reichs Chancellery," the guide said.

A contingent of Russian soldiers in long grey overcoats carrying a red wreath and swinging their free arms from side to side came marching past.

"It is forbidden to take photographs of military personnel," she said sharply, as an American raised a camera. "For those who do not have cameras I have postcards in the bus which you may buy with Westmarks."

"Would you like me to take a photograph of you and your children?" Spencer said to the blonde. He photographed them and walked back to the bus with them, deliberately attaching himself to the family group.

Several people bought postcards of the Russian war memorial in the bus. Spencer had no interest and started towards his seat.

"You do not wish a postcard?" the guide said.

"No, thank you."

"Please . . ."

"No. I . . ."

He was embarrassed that she seemed to be touting for business. Her face was tight with tension. To avoid a scene he said, "All right. Thank you." He paid and took a postcard back to his seat.

"We now go to a café," she was saying. "In this café you may buy tea or coffee or some drinks and you may pay in Westmarks. We will be there for thirty-five minutes."

Spencer had been holding the postcard in his lap. Now, as the bus pulled away, he looked down at it and frowned. It was not a picture of the Russian War Memorial. It appeared to be a view of a city park with a lake and a Tyrolean-style building in the foreground. He had never seen the place before. He turned it over but there was no writing on the other side. He looked more closely at the photograph and saw the faintest indentation in the paper. It was a small cross made in ballpoint just at the edge of the water. He glanced up at the tour guide, but she was sitting down with her back to him.

Why had she insisted on selling him a postcard unless this was some sort of message? Was this the place, where the cross was marked, where he was to meet Lange? And then he thought: Or was this the place where they wanted him to *believe* he was going to meet Lange? In any event, he had not the faintest idea where it was. The bus turned into Puschkin-allee. There were trees and grass on one side; on the other were houses that had survived the war. Some were substantial and he thought they must once have housed the burgesses of Berlin; now, he assumed, they would be split into apartments, the largest of which would go to Party officials.

The bus came to a stop. He found himself looking at the scene on his postcard, of a Tyrolean-style building standing by itself near the edge of a lake. The tour guide said, "We are now at the café. We have thirty-five minutes exactly, then we must all be back in the bus." They walked in little groups towards the building. Spencer stayed with the blonde and her children. The restaurant was on the first floor and they went up an outside staircase. Half way up he glanced towards the water.

He saw a group of chairs and tables. In summer they would be used by families out for a day in the sunshine. Now, on a grey winter's afternoon, there was only the bent figure of a man sitting at one of the tables.

"Excuse me," he said to the blonde. "I'll be back in a minute."

He went down the staircase and walked towards the table. The man was wrapped in a rug against the cold and wore a fur hat on his head. Slowly one old wattled hand rose and he spoke.

"Is that you, Spencer?"

Spencer paused. The tourists had gone into the café, the bus-driver was reading a paper and smoking. There was only this old man in the middle of the winter afternoon etched against the steel of the lake.

"Herr Lange?"

"Don't tell me you wouldn't have recognized me?" There

**130**

was something in the half-mocking tone of the voice that was familiar, but that was all.

The face was pinched and thin, the nose prominent, and there were weals down each cheek as though someone had taken a razor and slashed him and then the wounds had healed, leaving the scar tissue white and glaring.

"Herr Lange?" Spencer said again.

"Yes!" he said, irritated. "Come, sit down. Be honest, you wouldn't have known me, would you?"

"No."

"I suppose it's these." He tapped the scars. "Skin cancer. They have to burn it out. You got my message?"

"Message?"

"You make me repeat everything. I'm a very old man and I get tired easily. I sent you a postcard."

"The postcard. Yes."

There was a wheezing noise from the middle of the blanket and Spencer realized that Lange was laughing. "Did you get a fright?"

"Yes, I did."

"It had to be that way. The guide is a friend but I did not want to give her the responsibility of a verbal message. Our authorities are strict about some things and hers is a good job. So I thought of the postcard." He uncovered his hands and looked at his watch. "You've got thirty-five minutes, haven't you?"

Spencer looked at his watch. "Slightly less now. How do you know?"

"I live over there," Lange said, pointing to one of the substantial houses. "I watch these coaches every day. I watch the tourists spend their Westmarks on coffee and drinks and then they go away again. Oh, don't think I want to go with them. It's not that sort of encounter at all. But I sometimes come over on fine afternoons just to hear them talk, to see how they sound. Are they cheerful? Are they sad? We don't get too much news on this side of the Wall."

"Have you been here long?"

"Since the end of the war. I did rather well. You remember

**131**

I was with the *Rundfunk*? Well, they were glad to have me here and I managed to find a *raison d'être* with the Russians. I ended my career as head of the news services. *Ja,* they treated me well enough. Not bad for a boy from the bush in South-West Africa. We got along well enough. They're all right if you know how to treat them. Now, I received a message that you were coming this side of the Wall and would like to see me. I don't believe you've come all this way just to see an old sack of bones. I must say I thought twice about meeting you. What does Spencer want, I thought? Do I want to get mixed up with someone like that now? And then it seemed to me it could be easily done and I haven't so much to fill the time now that I can afford to pass up things of interest. So . . . please . . ."

Spencer began to talk, slowly at first and then more rapidly. He described exactly what had happened in London and for the first time he was grateful to be talking to someone who actually knew; to someone for whom the story did not need editing, who knew practically as much about the Berlin period as he did himself. When he had finished Lange said, "It's a dreadful story. Dreadful. But let me set your mind at rest in one direction. I had nothing to do with it."

"I didn't think you had."

"Nor was it Frau . . . Gutmann. That's how you remember her. She became Frau Lange, you know."

"You married her?"

"Yes. We married at the end of the war and came to live here. After the villa in Graf Speesstrasse was bombed."

"Did you have contacts here?"

"Not at all. But it seemed to me that with everyone fleeing West, there might be places to stay if one went in the opposite direction if one was in sympathy with the new master, which I was."

"How is Frau Gut . . . Frau Lange?"

"She died a year ago. So, who did you think it was?"

"Bruno." Spencer said it without emphasis, unwilling to show all his hand.

"You may be right."

Lange stared out towards the grey surface of the lake. It was formed by a bend of the River Spree and away to their left were the tower blocks and the buildings of the city, to their right an islet covered in large bare trees. There was a strange sadness about the place. Eventually he said, "I ask myself the same questions you have put to yourself. Why your house? And then, of course, the insignia, the leopards, from the uniform that Bruno wore so often. He was like a child with it, dressing up, primping. I must say, if I were you, I would certainly have thought of Bruno."

Just then a man in a check overcoat and cap strolled along the pathway and threw some pieces of bread to the swans. It was a picture that stabbed at Spencer. He could remember a day on the Thames at Teddington when he and Sue had thrown pieces of bread to the swans. There was something oddly familiar about the man but he walked on and Spencer turned once more to Lange.

"Bruno is a dangerous person," he was saying. "I think he is the only truly amoral person I have met in my life. Someone who literally does not know the difference between right and wrong. The war made him rich, you know."

"I'm not surprised."

"I don't know how he did it, but after we moved we saw a lot of him. That was in the bad time just after the war. No one had money, we were all cold and hungry. Except Bruno. I remember he had a wonderful coat. It was one of those coats wealthy people wore in the thirties. A great black coat with an astrakan collar. God knows where he got it from."

"Looted, probably. Once I found a shoe box under that big wardrobe in our room. It was filled with rings and necklaces, gold-rimmed spectacles, gold pens, anything valuable."

"I didn't know that."

"I didn't realize what it was myself till later on. At first I thought it belonged to Mrs Gutmann. I thought it had been put there for safe keeping. Eventually there were two shoe boxes. Later I realized how he got the stuff. That's why he was gone so often in those last days."

"Where was he looting?"

133

"In the bombed buildings."

Lange shook his old head slowly from side to side. Then in a querulous voice he said, "He never gave anything to his mother, you know. Not a pfennig. And he always had food: French cheeses, coffee, meat even. In those days it was like gold. I remember he came to our apartment once. Not here. We were living then in Kopenick. He had some *bratwurst*. This must have been late in 1945 in the winter. We hadn't seen a sausage for two or three months, not of that quality anyway. I suppose he had about half a kilo. His mother cooked it for him in the German way with apples and raisins—he even brought those, too. And he sat down and he ate everything, sausages, apples, even the last raisin, then he took a piece of our bread and wiped the pot." His hands jerked angrily under the rug. "I've never forgotten that. Whatever he does, he does for himself, and that means profit."

"But—in London—what did he have to gain?"

"Your house, Spencer. He used you. Another safe house, don't you see, like those of the *schili*. If the police get close, he will use you again. Let me tell you a story about Bruno. This happened some months after they put up the Wall. I don't believe in the Wall, by the way. You put a fence around people and they say, 'Why? I wonder what it's like on the other side. It may be better than here'. But anyway . . . the time I'm speaking of was when our Government decreed that it was forbidden to go into the West. You may remember there were escapes: people jumping from windows, flying over in small planes, swimming across the Wannsee. And, of course, the tunnels. There was one particular tunnel, I forget where it was exactly, somewhere near the checkpoint. It had been a series of cellars linked up beneath a row of houses that eventually led to a bomb shelter under the street, which in turn led to another series of cellars in the West. No one had to dig anything; it was there already. But no one knew about this tunnel because the people had all been evacuated."

Something stirred in Spencer's mind. "Had the houses been bombed?" he said.

"Some had been damaged, I think. Why do you ask?"

"I wondered, that's all."

"Please do not interrupt. Where was I? Oh, yes, the tunnels. This particular one was Bruno's tunnel and he was making a lot of money out of it. Each person who went through he charged. There were other escape organizations which did not want money, they were doing it from other motives. But in Bruno's tunnel you paid in advance, always with jewellery or valuables, never with money. Nearly five hundred people went through that tunnel. Then one day the authorities laid a trap and caught twenty people inside it and were able to close it for good."

"And you think that Bruno—?"

"Of course. Who else? I asked him about it. He didn't mind admitting it. I told you; he is an amoral person."

"Why did he do it?"

"For money. He told me that things were getting more and more difficult. He knew it would only be a matter of time before they found the tunnel, so he went to the authorities, told them about it as a loyal citizen and they paid him."

"So he was paid by both sides."

"That is true. You see what I mean about character?"

"Yes." Spencer looked at his watch. The time was running out. "What does he do now?"

"That I can't say. I know he lives in the West but he has no difficulty in coming into the East Zone. He used to come and visit his mother when he felt like a home-cooked meal. Sometimes he would even stay a day or two. I think the West German police may have been after him on these occasions. Once it was for nearly two weeks."

"What did he do after the tunnel was closed? How does he make his money?" He remembered the policemen Hoest in London telling him of the bank robberies and the bombings. Now he was hearing another side of Bruno's activities.

"He buys and sells. I believe he is what is called a middle man. And in this city if you have good contacts on either side of the Wall, life can be very sweet."

"What sort of things does he buy and sell?"

"I can't tell you everything he does because I don't know," Lange said. "But you in the West know we often suffer shortages, you are always writing about them. Well, say there is a shortage of cooking oil in the city and we need some quickly. We cannot wait for it to come from Rumania or Cuba. We must get it from the West."

"So you go to people like Bruno?"

Lange gave a small shrug. "*Force majeure*," he said.

"These contacts," Spencer said. "I can understand him having them in the West, but what about here?"

"We are only human, you know, Spencer."

"You mean he makes them through bribery?"

"Gifts might perhaps be a better word."

They stared at each other. Then Spencer heard voices and turned. The people from the restaurant were beginning to come down the staircase and make their way to the bus.

"Where can I find him?" he said.

"I wish I could help."

"Is there nothing you know? Not even a telephone number?"

"There may be. I can't say. My wife's address book is still at home."

"Will you look?"

"What are you going to do with him if you find him?"

Spencer did not reply.

"That is your business, anyway," Lange said.

"Yes. Will you look?"

The last of the tourists were queuing to get aboard.

"I always thought you were a sad case, Spencer. You did something wrong once and I knew you would live to regret it. I was right." He paused. "I'll look."

"How will you get it to me?"

"What's the name of your hotel?"

Spencer told him.

"I cannot promise anything."

Spencer rose and they shook hands. Lange's old skin was as cold as frozen meat. "I wish you good luck," he said. "I think you will need it."

Spencer ran to the bus. As it pulled away he looked out of the window. Lange was sitting where he had left him. Then slowly he rose to his feet and shuffled along the path by the lake.

*　　*　　*

Lilo was waiting for him when he reached the hotel. She was sitting on the edge of a chair in the lounge and behind her a group of people was watching a football match on television. She rose as he came in from the dark street and he thought how good she looked, tall, long-legged, the sweep of the blue suede coat to mid-calf and the high collar giving her a slender, almost an athletic look. He went towards her and they shook hands.

"Well?" she said.

"It has certainly been interesting."

"What happened?"

"Not here, with this going on." He indicated the television screen. "Let's go round to our . . . to the bar." The word "our" hung there for a second. They went to the Balkan restaurant. He was becoming familiar with the place and the waitress greeted him like an old friend. He felt at home there; territorial. They ordered gin-and-tonics.

"Cheers," he said.

"Good health "

He looked at her over the rim of his glass, thinking again what an attractive woman she was with her jet black hair cut straight across her eyebrows and her dark skin.

"Did you see him?"

"Yes. I didn't think I would, though. There was no message from you."

"I'm sorry about that. I was not certain right up to the last. I was working on it, and then it became too late for a message. He wouldn't say if he would see you or not."

"We were held up at the checkpoint. They kept us waiting for nearly half an hour and then they made us get out of the bus for an extra passport check."

"They do that sometimes. They do not like to refuse tourists, but they make it uncomfortable. How were you contacted?"

"Very cloak and dagger."

"Please?"

"I mean it was . . ." He groped for an explanation. "It was sinister. But then the whole bloody place is like that." He described how the tour guide had pressed the postcard on him. "I thought she was drumming up business. It was embarrassing. Then when I looked at it I saw it wasn't the Russian War Memorial at all." He described the area.

"It's the Treptower Park," she said. "You were afraid?"

"I suppose it was after the business at the checkpoint. And then I began to wonder where the postcard had originated. It crossed my mind it might have been sent by Bruno himself."

Her head jerked up and he could see a flash of anger in her eyes. "That means you do not trust me," she said.

"Don't be silly."

"*I* made the arrangements."

"I didn't mean it that way."

She said nothing, waiting for him to go on, but he could almost feel her animosity. "Well, anyway, that's where I met him, in the Treptower Park. The bus had stopped for refreshments; it was the same place as the picture. He was right where the cross was marked. God, he's old now. An old man wrapped up in a blanket with scars on his cheeks. But a lot of the old spirit was there. He's done very well. According to his lights."

"Yes," she said impatiently.

"He became head of the news service on their radio."

"Go on."

"Anyway, that's where we talked. Outside, by the lake."

"Well?"

"Well what?"

"What did he say? Did he tell you where Bruno was?"

"I'm afraid not."

"You mean he said nothing?"

"It was a waste of time."

"You were with him for thirty-five minutes and you got nothing from him?" There was a note of rising anger in her voice. "Do you expect me to believe that?"

"Why shouldn't you?"

The waitress was standing at the end of the little passage that led to the kitchen, watching them.

138

"You said you would co-operate with me on the story. You agreed that you would give me information."

"I have given you information. I have been co-operating."

"I go to the trouble of finding Lange for you and now you will not tell me anything."

"What can I tell you if there's nothing to tell?"

She got down off the bar stool and he could see her hands were trembling with rage. When he had first walked into the hotel she had been excited, anticipatory. Now the excitement had thrust her into anger. Her moods veered wildly.

"I will not help you more," she said, her English becoming ragged as her emotions grew more intense.

"Lilo, believe me! I would tell you if I could. We talked about Bruno. Lange told me about some of the things in the past. It's not my fault he doesn't know where Bruno is."

"I think you're lying," she said, and she turned on her heel and walked out.

He went back to his hotel room, poured himself a whisky and sat sipping it in his bath. He would have to be careful now. There were some things she could know and some things not, and he would have to watch where the line was drawn. When he had bathed he put on a towelling dressing-gown and went into the bedroom. He noticed a small square of white paper lying near the door and he knew it had not been there before. Someone must have pushed it under the door. He squatted down and turned it over. There was a telephone number on one side: 0041–82675. So the old man had managed after all. He sat on his bed, staring at the number; the telephone was only a few feet away. Should he phone now? His hand went out and he picked up the receiver.

"*Bitte?*" said the girl on the switchboard.

What was he going to say? How was he going to start the conversation?

He replaced the receiver and sat staring at it. First of all he would say, "Is that you, Bruno?" But what if Bruno did not answer? What if someone else answered? What if whoever answered said there was no one there by the name of Bruno? He would have to take the chance. He lifted the receiver again.

"*Bitte?*" said the voice. He gave her the number and heard her dialling. And then the ringing at the other end of the line. He had come out sweating from the bath, now he was cold and clammy. The phone went on ringing until finally he put down the receiver. As he did so there was a knock at the door. Lilo stood in the passage.

"I'm sorry. I've just had a bath," he said.

"May I come in."

"Let me get you a drink. Whisky?" He poured her one.

"I wanted to come to see you," she said, "to say I am sorry for what happened." She was calm now.

"Nothing happened."

"Yes, I was rude to you."

"You were disappointed, that's all. It's understandable."

"You are kind. I'm afraid I have a terrible temper. My father always said it would get me into trouble."

"And has it?"

She smiled. "I am in a strange man's bedroom—that could be trouble."

"Except I'm not a strange man."

"That's true." She kicked off her shoes and said, "May I sit on the bed?"

"Of course."

She curled her legs under her and sat against the headboard sipping her whisky.

"Have you eaten?" he said.

"No."

"Shall I order us something?"

"Do you like to drink?"

"Sometimes."

"I, too, sometimes." She held out her empty glass.

He brought her a new drink. "When we were talking in the bar I forgot something," she said.

"What's that?"

"To take notes."

"We can go over it again."

He repeated what he had told her about Lange and then she put down her notebook. There was a moment of silence while he searched for conversation then she said, "Last night you asked me to stay. Would you like me to stay tonight?"

"Yes." It slipped out before he could stop himself. He waited for the familiar feeling of self-disgust, of shame at his disloyalty, to sweep over him; instead his skin crawled with anticipatory pleasure.

"Excuse me a moment."

She went into the bathroom and closed the door. He heard the water running and in a little while she came out again. She had made herself a fresh drink, she had also taken off all her clothes except a half-slip. She was thin and high-breasted and he could see her rib-cage. She went back to the bed and he followed her. It was over quickly, too quickly, he thought, for her. The light was off and they lay in the glow from the city. He filled their glasses. She put her hand out, took his and said, "Was that all right for you?"

"Are you asking that on or off the record?" She smiled, and he bent and kissed her. "Of course!"

"Tell me what Lange said."

"About what?"

"You said there were things that Bruno had done."

He told her Lange's story about the escape tunnel and how Bruno had become a middle-man supplying shortages. "I'm sorry, there's no more to tell."

After a little while she looked at her watch. "It's late. I must go."

"I thought you were going to stay."

"I have stayed."

She swung her long legs off the bed and went into the bathroom. When she came out she said, "Do you want me to go on trying to put you in touch with Bruno?"

"Where would you start?"

"I'll have to think."

"Isn't there somewhere I can contact you?"

"I'm never there." She put her hand up to his face and touched it as she had the night before. It was a curiously maternal gesture. "Good-bye."

He sat on the bed for a long while after she had left. He

should have been elated, instead a feeling of sadness and loneliness came over him. He had another drink and then asked for Bruno's number again. As before, the telephone rang without answer.

Disgust settled on him like a cloak. What made it worse was that she had used him clinically and casually. She was an information gatherer—that is how she survived, how she made her living—and the method was of no concern.

He went to bed, but soon realized he was not going to be able to sleep. The anger remained but now, in the darkness, became diffused. Images fed it: Sue huddled by the door, the scream of Riemeck in the room. He twisted and turned, feeling the sweat break out on his body. Then, on top of those images came others: the woman police official at Checkpoint Charlie, the bus-guide pleading with him to buy a postcard, the wrapped, blanketed figure of Lange by the steel-grey lake, the old frozen hands, the scarred cheeks. And over everything the shadow of Bruno.

The more he learnt about Bruno, the more his anger and hatred grew. He knew now he was capable of destroying him, of rending and tearing him, of obliterating him. But at the same time he had to say to himself: be calm, be cool. Nothing would bring Sue back and he had his own life to live. He tried to force himself to sleep, to think of nothing, to make his mind a blank; but slowly, almost of their own volition, other images began to form. He was back in Berlin during the war, during those final days, when he had seen Bruno for the last time; the time he always tried to keep out of his thoughts.

\*　　\*　　\*

It was spring, bitterly cold, and in the house in Graf Spee-strasse they wore four and five layers of clothing for there was no fuel left to heat the building. There had been twenty successive night raids by Mosquito bombers and most of that part of Berlin had been reduced to empty shells and rubble. But people still survived, houses still survived, life went on. He remembered that day very clearly.

Lange had recently come in from working the night shift

142

on the news-desk in the *Rundfunk* and they were having lunch at the kitchen table—if it could be called lunch. Lange and Bruno were arguing, as they argued almost every day now.

"The trouble with you, Lange, is that you have a gloomy outlook. You pretend to be humorous but you are a pessimist."

"I prefer to call it a realist."

"You think we will all be finished. Wiped out. That is not so."

"How the hell do you know?" He lit a cigarette and Bruno waved the smoke away."

"Because there is going to be peace."

"Peace!" Lange said. "You mean unconditional surrender."

"No, I do not mean that."

"Who do you think is going to make peace with Germany?"

"I tell you, von Runstedt has already made an offer to Eisenhower for an honourable peace."

"I don't believe it."

"You never believe anything. That is your trouble. You are a cynic."

"Where do you get this information from?"

"It's all over Berlin."

"I haven't heard it."

"And not only that. Negotiations have begun with the British Embassy in Stockholm."

"Oh, God, that story!"

"I tell you it will be an honourable peace. The German Army will stop fighting. Everything will stop. And we will remain on our lines."

"If you believe that, you'll believe anything."

"It's true."

"Then tell me why the Government is leaving Berlin?"

"That's a lie."

"In the major departments 60 per cent of the staff have been dismissed. The men have been ordered to join the Home Guard. The women have been advised to quote disappear unquote."

"What does disappear mean?"

"It means find a place of safety. And part of the remainder have been sent straight away to emergency headquarters."

"That's the sort of rumour that undermines morale," Bruno said.

"Listen, the Foreign Press Club is to be moved to Mulhausen. The diplomats go to Wildungen. And Supreme Headquarters to Meiningen. Does that sound as though we're about to have peace?"

A calculating look came over Bruno's face. After a moment he said, "Is this really true?"

"Of course it's true."

Spencer had had enough of their arguing. He left the house and walked towards the Tiergarten in the bitter spring wind. It was too early to go to Annie's apartment because she worked in a munitions factory at night and slept during the morning, usually getting up about two o'clock. As a child he had seen picture books of the First World War, of the battlefields around the Somme and Ypres. Pictures of mud and torn trees, stunted trunks and splintered branches. Now as he walked through the Tiergarten he was vividly reminded of them. The park looked as though it were part of a moon landscape; cratered and torn. And yet on those trees that remained there were buds, and new leaves.

He walked on and came to the Brandenburg Gate. Unter den Linden had been hit by the raid the previous night and fires were still burning along its length. He turned away from it and walked on down to the Potsdamerplatz past piles of rubble and burst water mains, picking his way through the desolation; he hardly saw it now.

He crossed Leipzigerstrasse and entered an area of smaller streets lined with apartment buildings, some in ruins, some still standing, and in these there was evidence of life going on as usual; in many windows washing had been put out to dry. He was not too far from Annie's flat. He thought of her, warm and relaxed in the big double bed. He thought of waking her, of himself getting between the still-warm sheets. He felt excited and turned his steps towards her.

At that moment the sirens went and almost immediately he

144

could hear the batteries of anti-aircraft guns in the south-west sector of the city. He began to cast around for somewhere he could take cover. He saw an arrow directing him to the nearest shelter, but the way was blocked. The gunfire came nearer as batteries close to the centre of the city opened up. He could hear above the sharp crack-crack-crack of the guns the crr-ump of bombs. He seemed to be the only person in the derelict street. The bombs came nearer. He began to run.

He had no idea where he was running, only that movement was better than inaction. He came to the end of a partially ruined apartment block and saw what looked like an opening into a basement. He ran down a flight of steps and found himself in what had once been the laundry area. It had no wall at the back and did not seem very safe. But a doorway led away from it into the bowels of the building and he pushed past fallen masonry and found himself in a network of passageways filled with electricity cables and central-heating pipes.

Bombs were falling very close now. One landed with a terrible explosion about a hundred metres ahead of him. It shook the building and brought down dust and plaster. He turned and ran back along the passageway until he came to the laundry. As he reached it a bomb exploded in the street outside. He felt rather than heard the explosion.

When he regained consciousness he thought he was paralysed. He could not move the lower part of his body. He was lying on a heap of fallen masonry and when he turned his head he could see that a baulk of timber was trapping his legs. Slowly he twisted from side to side and took in his surroundings. The bomb had blown out another wall and daylight was streaming in but because there was no sun he could not tell what time of day it was. It was very quiet; there were no guns and no bombs and it sounded as though the raid was long over. He felt something sticky on his cheek and put up his hand, touched it and saw that it was blood. He felt the wound itself above his right ear. He had no idea how bad it was but it no longer seemed to be bleeding. He realized he must have been unconscious for several hours.

As his senses returned he began to shiver in the cold and

145

knew he would not survive unless he managed to free himself or someone came to help. He struggled, but the beam was too heavy. He shouted, his voice echoing through the ruined building. And then, from somewhere nearby, he heard an answering call.

He was not certain from which direction it came, so he shouted again, and again he was answered. The voice came from somewhere over his left shoulder. He managed to twist round until he was facing in the correct direction. Just then a pale sun broke through the cloud layer and lit the interior of the building with mote-filled shafts. At first, because of the dust, he could make out very little, and then he saw her, about ten metres from him. All he could see was the top part of her body. She was covered in dust, her hair matted.

"Help me," she said.

"Are you badly hurt?" he called.

"Help me." Her voice was shrill with hysteria.

"I can't move. Are you badly hurt?"

"Can't you help me?"

"Someone will come along soon."

"Oh, my God!" she said, and then she screamed, the sound bouncing and echoing off the broken walls.

"Are you in pain?" he said.

She ignored all his questions but from what he could make out she seemed to be an elderly woman with a large round face and plump arms. "Can you come over here?" he said. "If you can come over here and help me with this beam . . ."

"I can't move!" she shrieked. "Look!"

She raised both her arms and moved them and he saw that the lower portion of her body was buried in rubble. There was silence as they took stock of each other's positions. Neither could free their legs. They were not able to help each other.

"I'm cold," she said.

He was shaking with cold, too.

"Where were you when the bomb fell?" he said, his teeth chattering.

"In my apartment."

"Where was that?"

146

"On the first floor."

So she had come plunging down from the first floor to the basement.

"What is your name?" He did not find it odd that he, a youth, was comforting someone old enough to be his grandmother.

"I am Mrs Mentzel."

"What about your husband. Won't he look for you?"

"My husband died years ago. Who are you? You sound foreign."

"I was born in England."

"He was a cheese importer."

"Who?"

"My husband. He imported from all over: Pont l'Evêque, Esrom, Bel Paese, Gruyère, Reblochon, Carre de l'Est." Her voice trailed away. "On Saturdays he always brought home something nice. A Brie. A Bleu de Bresse, just ready." She began to cry.

"They can't be too long," he said, but he didn't believe it himself. He had seen bodies stiff and dead on bombed sites before. There were just too many injured; not all could be rescued in time.

"What's that?" she said.

"What?"

There was a noise of falling masonry and he turned to look. As he did so she screamed again. At first all he could make out was a shadow, black against the sky, then it moved a few paces towards them. He thought it was a dog, then he realized that no dog he had ever seen was as large as this. The animal came down a slope of rubble, placing one paw delicately after another, sending little trickles of pebbles ahead of it. It came through a shaft of sunlight and he saw that it was not a dog. He was looking at a North American timber wolf, a female, in an emaciated condition. She was coloured dark grey, almost sable on her shoulders, lightening towards her belly. Her fur was dull and her ribs were clearly visible. She was in a highly nervous state. Until a week before she had been in a den created for her and several other wolves in the Zoo, but the

**147**

bombing had smashed down the wire enclosures and had killed all the others of her pack. She was the sole survivor. For two days she had not eaten. Then in a bombed building she had made a meal from the carcass of a cat. But there had been nothing else for nearly four days and she was starving.

Mrs Mentzel screamed again and the wolf checked, growling softly all the time.

"Get away!" Spencer shouted.

But the animal came on, taking one or two more small steps. Spencer picked up half a brick and with all his strength he flung it at her. It smacked into what must once have been the enamel side of a cooker, for it made a tremendous clanging. In a flash the wolf had whisked up the slope and was gone.

Mrs Mentzel was crying hysterically and he said, "It's all right now, it's gone."

"Oh, my God!" she said. "Oh, my God!"

"It's gone."

"What was it?"

"A dog."

"A dog?"

He was thinking of what he had heard about the bombing of the Zoo: of the snakes and crocodiles said to lurk in the bush near the canal, of the tiger in the restaurant. It had been a joke then.

Suddenly he realized that she was no longer crying. "Don't worry," he said. "They'll soon come to fetch us." She did not reply and her head appeared to be lolling forward as though she were unconscious or dead.

He was alone again. He began to struggle with renewed vigour, but the beam resisted all his efforts and finally, exhausted, he collapsed on his stomach.

Would it be back? Since his childhood he had been frightened of wolves. They had appeared in the nursery stories, laying a shadow of terror over them; and then at school there had been novels and short stories about wolves that came down from the mountains in a bad winter, of the *troika* rushing through the snow and the old and weak being thrown out to appease the slavering pack.

148

The day was dying when he woke for the second time. Through the broken wall he could see the blood red clouds of sunset. He was stiff and frozen and found it difficult to move. Then he heard a noise. It was the slithering trickle of small stones, this time louder than on the previous occasion, and he knew that the wolf had come back. He was facing away from the sounds and desperately, as a child would, he wanted to close his eyes and pull blankets over his head. Instead he forced himself to face it. But it was not there. The slope of masonry leading up to the broken wall was bare.

He shifted to look at Mrs Mentzel. The figure of a man was squatting next to her and looked to be stroking one of her hands. A feeling of enormous relief came over Spencer. It must, he thought, be one of the *Hilfdienst* who had found them at last and was comforting the old woman. He opened his mouth to call when suddenly Mrs Mentzel regained consciousness and screamed. She screamed again and again and beat the man with her other hand. He released her, scooped up a piece of rubble twice the size of an ordinary house brick and, with her scream still ringing through the building, brought it down with all his force on her head. He stood there for a second, as though waiting to hit her again, but he must have been satisfied that she was dead, for he threw the lump of masonry to one side and bent again to his task, which Spencer had assumed to be one of soothing a frightened old woman by stroking her hands. Instead, as he tugged and tugged at the finger, Spencer could see that he was, in fact, wrenching off the rings embedded in the plump flesh.

He lay very still. Even the horror of what he had seen could not blot out the fear that he would be next, not from anything valuable he owned, but simply because he had been a witness. The man struggled for some time before he managed to pull the last of the rings off. Like many women at that time, she was wearing all the jewellery she had as a form of safety. At last he stood up, put the rings in the pocket of his coat and then looked about him as though searching for other victims. He saw Spencer. He picked up a second lump of concrete and came across the rubble. Spencer closed his eyes, pretending to be dead. Then the man stopped. "Johnnie!" he said softly.

Spencer's eyes snapped open and he looked up into Bruno's face.

"My God, Johnnie, we were worried!" Bruno said, dropping the concrete lump. "We've been looking for you. What happened?"

It was as though the old woman's murder had never taken place.

"Are you all right?"

"My legs . . ."

"Don't worry. We'll have that off in a moment." But he made no move to shift the beam. He squatted there, looking down. "Where did you go?"

"For a walk. To the Brandenburg Gate and then down here. I was caught in a raid. Can you get it off my legs?"

"Yes. Sure. In a minute. Let me just see, I don't want to hurt you or make it worse, you know." But instead of looking at the beam he was looking at Spencer. Then he said, "Did you see what happened over there?" and he gave a slight twitch of his head.

Spencer did not reply.

"It was the kindest thing to do, you know. I tried to move her, but it was impossible. She was trapped."

Spencer stared at him. He could have pointed out that had Bruno gone for help the *Hilfdienst* could soon have shifted the rubble.

"I mean, that's what you would do to an animal, isn't it? When it hurts itself badly and there is no way it can recover. It's a kindness to put it out of its misery. And that's all I did. What do you say, Johnnie?"

Spencer could find no words. Bruno picked up a piece of concrete, larger than his fist, and said, "You think I should have gone for help? Let me ask you where? Don't you realize how bad the raid was? There's almost nothing left in this part of town. Do you think you can just go out into the street and call for help and help will come? I tell you, there would have been no help. She would have died tonight. If she hadn't died

150

from her wounds she would have died from cold. Instead of looking at me like that you should be pleased that I acted like a man."

Spencer thought of Mrs Mentzel with her plump face and her plump fingers covered with rings; and of her husband who imported cheeses and always brought home something nice on a Saturday night. And he thought of the terror she had undergone, not only from the bombing but from the wolf, and how pleased she must have been to see Bruno; someone come to save her at last.

"You want to know why I took her rings?" Bruno said. "I'll tell you why. Ask yourself what good would they have been to her? You can't take rings up there, you know." He pointed skywards. "Anyway, where did she get all those rings? One on every finger. Is that how women dress? Rubbish! You can't tell me that. A ring on every finger! Stolen, probably. That's more like it. Stolen from someone else. Looted, maybe. You can get the death sentence for looting, you know." He had worked himself up into a rage. Then he paused as though realizing what he had said and to whom it applied. "Of course, only if the authorities know about it. Do you think they will find out?"

"Help me!" Spencer said.

Bruno moved the concrete from one hand to the other. "Everybody does it. You know that? Everybody!"

"Help me with the beam."

"That's just it, Johnnie. If I help you, how do I know you won't harm me?"

"I promise."

"Yes, now, when things are bad for you, you promise. But maybe tomorrow when you are feeling better, then you forget your promise, isn't it?"

"I won't forget it."

"You know, Johnnie, you and me could have been friends."

"We are friends."

"I mean real friends. We would have been if it hadn't been for Lange. I warned you about him. He's an unhealthy type. We don't want his type here in Germany."

"I can't feel my legs any more."

Bruno squatted there, seemingly deep in thought, moving the lump of concrete from one hand to the other.

"What am I to do with you, Johnnie?" he said.

At that moment there was a growl from above them. They looked up and there was the wolf.

"My God," Bruno said. "What's that?"

"A wolf. It must have escaped from the Zoo. It was here before."

"What does it want?"

"It's starving."

"I must get out of here."

"For God's sake, help me! Throw something."

Bruno hurled the concrete at it. It smashed into the rubble to the right of the animal, but this time the wolf controlled her fear. She sprang to one side, the growl rising in pitch. Instead of turning and running, she came down towards them. It was enough for Bruno. He turned and ran headlong over the rubble, slipping and scrambling.

"Bruno!" Spencer shouted. "Bruno!" But all he could hear were Bruno's running footsteps in the street outside.

The wolf stood on the pile of rubble. She had been smelling blood for several hours and finally her needs had overcome her fear. Spencer watched her as he groped for something to throw. She came down the broken slope towards him. He picked up a piece of plaster and hurled it at her. It hit her on the side but had no force. She stopped. Her lips were drawn back, revealing her long teeth, and she was snarling continuously.

She turned away from Spencer and slowly, as though suspecting something was going to attack her, she advanced on the dead torso of Mrs Mentzel. Spencer threw one piece of plaster after another, but the wolf had grown used to them now and hardly noticed as they fell around her. She stopped several paces from Mrs Mentzel and then, as though having made up her mind, she darted forward and snatched at one of the hands, tearing away the flesh below the thumb, biting off the fingers. She retreated. Stopped. Stood. Watched. There was no reaction from the old lady's body. The wolf knew now that

152

it was safe. Spencer watched her go forward again, but this time with confidence. He knew what was going to happen and he buried his head in his hands, trying to cover his ears as well as the wolf settled down to feed.

And that is how they found him two hours later, stiff with cold, almost dead. When they asked him what had happened to the woman's body he said he didn't know.

"Don't ask him questions," one of the *Hilfdienst* officers said. "Can't you see he's almost a goner?" They put him on a stretcher and carried him away.

They kept him in hospital for two days, until his legs were better, then they let him go. During that time he came to a decision: Bruno must clearly think him dead so why not *be* dead. He decided not to go back to the villa in Graf Spee-strasse, but instead to go to Annie.

In the two days he had been in hospital there was almost continuous bombing and when he reached the area in which she lived he saw that her apartment block had been hit and one of the corners of the building had been demolished. He ran into the main entrance. The elevators were not working and there was dust and plaster everywhere and great cracks in the walls. He climbed the six flights on painful legs and hammered at her door. It opened almost instantly. They held each other desperately for a moment and through her tears she said, "I thought you were dead". They went into the room and closed the door behind them, still holding onto each other as though by losing physical contact they might be wrenched apart and never find each other again.

"When you didn't come I went to the villa," she said. "The whole street had gone except for a couple of houses. Your house is a pile of rubble. I thought you might be under it but the wardens said there was no one. Then I thought instead of looking for you I'd sit tight. You knew where the apartment was. If you were all right you'd come. I haven't been out for nearly forty-eight hours." She enveloped him in her arms, smiled and said, "This surely calls for a celebration." She fetched a bottle of schnapps from the kitchen and poured him a glass and one for herself. He had tasted the oily liquor at the house in Charlottenburg with Astley and Richards and the first time it had almost made him gag. Now the adrenalin was flowing so quickly through his veins that he hardly tasted it.

"Tell me what happened," she said. They were sitting together on a small sofa. She was holding his hands. He turned to look at her and she moved her head and said, "Don't look at me." Her skin was sallow, her eyes puffy, her hair lank and uncombed. "Wait, before you tell me, give me a minute." She went to the bathroom and they talked through the door. She told him about the raid in which her apartment building was hit. Several tenants on the opposite side had been killed. After ten minutes she came out and rejoined him. She was wearing a flowered house-coat, her hair was done and her face was made up. She looked more in possession of herself. "Now," she said. "What happened?"

Spencer told her. He left nothing out. When he'd finished she whispered, "My God!" and sat trying to assimilate what she had heard. She asked him several times about his legs and he reassured her. And then about the old woman. She never mentioned the wolf, it was as though she did not want to think about it.

After a while, when she had recovered, she gave him another drink and said, "Listen, I've been doing a lot of thinking. You can't go back to Graf Speestrasse because the house doesn't exist any more. And if you go to the authorities you'll be sent to fight the Russians and they're only eighty kilometres away. People say they're going to reach Berlin before the British or the Americans. You could stay here with me, but what happens when the Russians get here? I know what they'll do to me. But God knows what they'll do to you. I figure it's best for you to get back to the camp and be there when the Allies get there. That way no one need know."

Spencer thought of the thousands of refugees making their way westwards, choking the roads and the railways.

"You've got to have a special pass to travel on the trains."

"That's what I've been figuring. I want to get out too. I've got a car. It's not much, but it goes. And I've got a friend from my conservatorium days who lives in Bremen. She'll give me a bed. And we'll be near each other. Then after you're released . . ." Her voice faded away.

"What?"

"We mustn't think about that. No one knows what the future holds."

Had Spencer been older he would have noticed the change in her. His absence and the thought of his death had broken down the barrier which her age and caution had caused her to place between them. Until then she had enjoyed their affair on her terms, had been touched at the depth of his feelings for her but had managed to restrain her own, knowing that what was happening had no future. Each moment was to be savoured for itself. But when he had not come, when she had seen the ruin of the house in Graf Speestrasse, when she had sat hour after hour in her apartment thinking of him dead, of his limbs broken, shorn from his body, a change had come over her. She had longed for him, for his beauty and his companion-ship, for his love. All her pent-up emotions, which had never expressed themselves in Herr Beckmann's company, were released. She knew she was a middle-aged woman pretending to be nineteen, that ahead lay only emotional danger, but she could not help herself. She loved him with all the passion and tenderness of which she was capable.

They spent the night in the big double bed and the following morning early she took him to the underground garage two streets away where she kept her little Fiat Topolino. The car had two bucket seats and a small space behind them for luggage. He had nothing and she took with her only a small leather travelling bag, a present from Herr Beckmann. The rest of the space was taken up by three jerrycans of petrol which she had been hoarding against such a contingency.

They left Berlin as dawn was breaking and drove out on the Potsdam Chausee. The road surface was pockmarked with bomb craters and was strewn by burnt-out trucks and cars caught by Allied fighter-bombers. There was also the usual quota of refugees from the east pushing their belongings in prams or riding bicycles pulling small carts. The tiny Topolino was the ideal car for the journey as it was small enough to squeeze through gaps in the traffic and by the time they reached Wolfsburg, the road was almost clear. They turned towards Celle and there the gearbox broke down and they could only travel in third. The Hanover–Bremen autobahn was being strafed by low-flying Spitfires and Annie said, "We must get off this, can you work something out on the map?"

They turned on to a series of small roads that kept them parallel with the autobahn but south of the Weser. Spencer sat with the road map on his knees, trying to navigate as well as watch out for aircraft. They had not very far to go to Bremen when the fighters finally found them. Approaching Bassum he looked back and saw three Spitfires flying low up the road towards them.

"Planes!" he shouted. "Behind us!"

"There's a lane!" she said.

He saw a small road leading into a pine forest that would give them perfect shelter. She put her foot down to the floor-boards, but they were going up a small hill and being in third gear the engine could not take it. The car spluttered and stalled. At that moment the first Spitfire was thundering in at treetop height behind them. At five hundred metres it started pumping machine-gun and cannon fire from its wings. As Spencer looked back he could see the flashes. The explosions ripped up the road in two lines then the car was engulfed and hot metal was screeching past his face. He opened the door and flung himself out into a ditch. He waited for Annie to jump out on the opposite side. But nothing happened. The planes flew on, not bothering to turn, not bothering with the Topolino any more, looking for bigger game. He shouted at her. There was no reply. He got out of the ditch and ran back to the car. She lay over the wheel, arterial blood dripping down onto the floor. A fragment from a cannon shell had severed her spinal cord at the base of her neck and she was dead.

Three days later he reached the prisoner-of-war camp. He had buried Annie as best he could, scraping a grave for her in the pine forest with one end of the starting handle, lining it with fir branches and placing her on them as though in a cata-falque. Then he covered her body with more branches and took a private farewell.

Her death changed him. He had loved her with the simpli-city of youth; now she had been taken from him. After the first shock wore off it was as though the soft malleable clay of his personality had gone through fire in a kiln and come out hard and tough and not easily broken.

The camp was as he remembered it, except for one vital difference: it was now in the hands of the prisoners and the *Kommandantur* was a smoke-blackened shell. As he went up the road towards it he found himself part of a mob of prisoners, some armed with carbines, some with bayonets, some with heavy sticks, who were clearly in charge both of the camp and the surrounding countryside. Not a German was in sight. Many of the men were drunk. Some lay on the ground near the huts and Spencer could not tell whether they were sleeping it off or whether they were dead.

He learned that the camp authorities had left several days before and that the Allies were expected within twenty-four hours. He made his way to his old hut. He didn't care now whether there was a bunk for him or not. If the Allies were as close as they were said to be, everything would change, every-thing would be reorganized when they arrived. There was no one in the room and he noticed that his bunk was bare of blankets or palliasse; he would have somewhere to sleep after all. He looked round calmly at the familiar features, the table, the benches, the chairs, the stove; everything was filthy, nothing had been washed up; nothing had been cleaned. It was as though freedom had given his former hutmates the opportunity of living as they would have wished. He looked out of the window and saw that in places the wire had been cut and one or two of the guard towers were now being patrolled by a former prisoner.

He heard a sound behind him and turned—and there was Campbell. "Well," the big stoker said. "Well, well, look who's back!" He kicked the door closed behind him and came across the hut. "So you couldna do without me."

From the time he had left Berlin Spencer knew that this moment had been inevitable. He slipped his hand inside his heavy seaman's coat and came out with a screwdriver, part of the Topolino's tool kit. The two nights he had spent on the road since Annie's death he had used to sharpen it on whatever stone was handy; now in the dull afternoon light from the window it gleamed like the point of a needle. He held it low, aiming at Campbell's stomach.

"Touch me," he said, "and I'll kill you."

Campbell blinked. There was something different about the pretty boy he'd wanted so badly some months before. He took another step forward as though to test him but Spencer did not move, not even an eyelid. He stood there calmly waiting to disembowel the Scot.

"My Gawd," Campbell whispered. "I believe you would!" He backed away towards the door and went out into the compound.

The following morning Allied tanks came up the road to the camp and the war, for all of them, was finally over.

*     *     *

When Spencer awoke the next morning in his Berlin hotel the effects of the sleeping pill had made him thick-headed and he thought at first that the memories were part of a nightmare and then he remembered lying awake and sweating, trying not to think, but being forced to remember not only Bruno but Annie and Campbell, and he realized, with a sense of shock that the one person of whom he should be thinking, on whom his whole mind should be concentrating had had no place in his thoughts—Sue. Again the picture flashed into his mind of the tangled limbs by the front door, Sue on her side, her arm flung out, the great bulge of her belly, the pattern of red holes across her chest; but the anger did not spurt; it had been damped down by other thoughts and other emotions. He was in the grip of Berlin again. There was layer upon layer into which he had dug and now the layers threatened to bury him.

His eyes fell on the telephone number which Lange had

sent him and he seemed to feel cold fingers touch his bowels at the thought of telephoning Bruno. The picture of the cellar, the brutality, remained vivid and had somehow undermined his will. He decided to leave it until after breakfast. Or on the other hand, he told himself angrily, it was simply the effects of the pill. He flung back the covers and went into the bathroom and had a boiling hot shower followed by an ice cold one and felt better. It was well after ten o'clock by the time he was dressed, and breakfast was over, so he went to the *konditorei* next door and had coffee and a roll. He was standing at the cash desk waiting to pay when out of the corner of his eye he saw something that caught his attention. Through the big window he glimpsed Lilo coming out of the hotel and crossing the road to her car. The woman behind the cash desk had turned to the waitress to check something on the bill and by the time he had paid, Lilo was in her car. He shouted but she did not hear him. An empty taxi was leaving the hotel and Spencer told the driver to follow the blue Manta.

They crossed the centre of town and then drove along the Bismarck-strasse. Finally she turned off into a quiet suburban street in Charlottenburg and parked. Spencer stopped the taxi a little short of her car and followed her to the entrance of a small apartment block.

She must have felt his presence for she turned, startled. When she saw who it was her eyes widened with anger. "You followed me! How dare you come here! How dare you spy on me!"

"I saw you at the hotel. You came to see me."

"You should not have come here! This is my private life! It is nothing to do with you."

"I'm not prying into your private life."

Abruptly she moved away from the door and stood with her back to the letter-boxes. It was as though she was saying: "Keep away from me."

"I'm not going to harm you," he said. "You wanted to see me. I wanted to see you."

She paused and then reluctantly said, "Now that you're here, you'd better come up."

159

He put out his hand, indicating that she should go first, but she stood her ground. He opened the street door and went in. "The first floor," she said. "On the left."

He went up the stairs to the landing. As on the ground floor there were two apartments, one left, one right. She unlocked the door on the left and said, "Please go in, I will be with you in a minute." She walked across to the other apartment, rang the bell and went in. A moment later she came out again carrying a baby boy of about eighteen months. He was a beautiful child with fair hair and blue eyes. He was clutching a panda almost as big as himself.

"This is Peter," she said, and the hostility seemed to have vanished.

Spencer was as surprised now as she had been a few minutes before. "Hello, Peter," he said.

She closed the apartment door behind her. "It's time for his sleep. I must put him down. Please wait in the sitting-room."

But he followed her into the child's bedroom. "Don't worry, I've seen babies changed before." The child reminded him of Dick, the same fair skin, the same blue eyes. He felt a wrench of longing and sadness, and above all, a need to communicate. For weeks he had been unable to communicate on a domestic level. Ever since Sue's death he had been a person within a person. But now everything was shaking loose. And Lilo was the only person he had; Lilo, who was a total enigma.

"You've never changed one," she said, fetching a fresh cotton wool pad and beginning to unbutton Peter's overpants.

"Many times."

"But you didn't have children."

"A boy like Peter."

"You didn't tell me. How can I write a story about you if I do not have all the facts?"

For the hundredth time he wondered whether she was lying but he let it pass.

"His name was Dick," he said briefly. "He died."

She swung to look at him, frowning. "How old was he?"

"Grown up, with a family."

"How did it happen?"

"Car accident."

She bent and went on with what she was doing. "When they're very young you look after them almost hour by hour," he said, more to himself than to her. "You try to guess what they'll do, what harm they can come to. Can they reach that window? Can they pull that cupboard onto themselves? Can they get out of that door? Down that flight of steps? Across that road? You try and see every eventuality and then, just when they're grown up and beginning to reap the benefits of having got there . . . bang! Out like a candle." He stared from the window. "It wasn't only Dick. His wife and child were in the car. They were also killed."

He turned to look at her again and was astonished to see she was crying. The tears simply slid halfway down her cheeks and fell onto the cot.

"Lilo."

"I'm sorry. Forgive me."

"I shouldn't have talked like that."

"It reminded me of someone else."

"Look, I'll leave you. I'll go into the sitting-room."

"No. Keep me company."

He felt drawn to her then for the first time on a basis which was not sexual.

She gathered up the debris and removed it to the bathroom. The baby lay on his back, clean and gurgling. Spencer picked him up and carried him to the window. Peter pointed.

"What's that?" Spencer said. "A tree? Yes, that's what it is, a tree."

Lilo came back. "This is the time his father used to like him. When he was clean and smelling nice." She held out her arms, took him back and tucked him in his cot.

"I'm going to make some coffee," she said, closing the door behind them.

He followed her into the small modern kitchen. "Does his father ever see him or is it a total break?"

She turned away to fill the kettle. "Total."

"Perhaps that's best."

They took their coffee into the sitting-room. It was a

pleasant, unassuming room. A lot of the furniture was cheap veneer but there was an angle sofa in oatmeal tweed on a deep brown carpet that gave it a focus. She turned and kissed him on the lips and put her free hand up in a gesture that he now thought characteristic, and touched his face. "Sit over there."

"What have you been doing?" he said.

She sipped at the smoky surface of the coffee and then said, "Finding out more about your friend Bruno."

"Oh?"

"I have a good contact in the police."

Again he wondered if she was lying. And then he thought: "I don't care. For just these few moments, I don't care."

"What did you find out?" he said.

The telephone rang. It was on a table in the corner of the room. "Excuse me, please," she said. She stood with her back to him, cupping the receiver in her hand so that he would not hear. In any case, the German was too rapid for him to follow. At first she seemed to be listening and then she spoke swiftly and jerkily, as though arguing. Once or twice she turned to look at him and then quickly turned back again. When she put down the receiver she looked agitated. "I'm sorry," she said. "I must ask you to leave now."

"I hoped . . ."

"There is someone coming."

"I see."

"It is important for me."

"Is it about Gutmann?"

"No, it is another matter."

"Your husband?"

"No."

He rose. "When will I see you?"

"I will telephone to you."

It was the same phrase she had used several times before. He went out into the misty morning. In the street he hesitated and look towards her apartment. He could just see her shape in the window looking down at him. He raised his hand to wave but she did not acknowledge it. He hadn't walked more than a hundred metres before he picked up a taxi. As it turned into Bismarck-strasse a blue Volkswagen left its parking place and turned after it, but he did not notice it.

At the hotel he went to the telephonist in her small cubby hole near the cloakroom.

"I'd like you to find out a telephone number for me. A Frau Lilo Essenbach. The address is in Charlottenburg."

The telephonist looked in the directory, then shook her head.

"Could you try Inquiries?"

She dialled, talked for a moment, then said, "They do not have a Frau Lilo Essenbach."

"Are you sure?"

"*They* are sure."

"Tell them it may be a new number or even ex-directory."

She spoke again. "No one by that name."

"Thank you."

The room was a cage and he prowled around it like an animal, his mind a jumble of conflicting thoughts: where the hell did she fit in? There was only one way to find out. He asked for the number that Lange had given him. This time there was the click of a receiver being lifted.

"Hello?" he said. "Hello?"

There was silence at the other end.

"Hello!" There was another click as the receiver was replaced. He sat on the edge of the bed, his skin crawling. He got through again but the telephone rang and rang until he finally put it down. He was half way through the door when the phone rang. He spun round and looked at it, hypnotized. Then he went back and picked it up.

It was Willi and he sounded frightened. "I have some information," he said.

"What sort of information?"

"You wish to find Bruno, not so?"

"You know that."

"It is about this matter."

Spencer felt his heart begin to race. "Where are you?"

"At the house."

"I'll come there."

"No."

"All right, you come here."

"That is not possible."

"All right, where then?"

"Somewhere open. The Zoo."

"In this weather? We'd freeze."

"You choose, please."

There was only one "open" place that he knew. "What about the Europa Centre? By the ice rink?"

There was a pause. "Yes, all right. In two hours. Bring some marks. A lot of marks." The phone went dead.

Spencer replaced the receiver and turned. Lilo was standing in the open doorway of the room.

He thought she looked lovelier than he had ever seen her: the black bar of her fringe cutting across and framing the olive skin of her face, the head itself framed by the high collar of her blue suede coat. Yet there was an uneasiness that had not existed before.

"Have you any of that whisky left?" she said lightly.

"About half a bottle." It was a little early in the day for whisky, he thought.

She took off her coat and her shoes and sat against the headboard of the bed, her long legs curled up underneath her, as she had before. It seemed impossible that she would lie to him, and yet she had, he wondered how many times, perhaps everything was a lie.

"I was going to telephone to apologize," she said.

"What for?"

"For today at the apartment, and then I thought it would be nicer to see you."

There was silence for a few moments and he said, "How's Peter?"

Her eyes slid away from him as though it was a subject she did not want to discuss and she said, "He is with my mother."

They talked desultorily for a few minutes, then the conversation languished. He gave her another whisky. Suddenly she said, "John, who were you speaking to?"

"When."

"Now, when I came."

"Just the desk."

She did not comment for a moment and then she said, "I am afraid for you."

"You needn't be."

"This is a very complex situation." He heard echoes of Hoest's voice in London. "If you know anything . . ."

"For Christ's sake, I've told you!" He was angry with her now; angry with her for lying, but basically angry with her for not being the person he wanted her to be. "What makes you think I've got anything to hide?"

She laughed without humour. "I will tell you. I think you found out something from Herr Lange; something that you have not wished to tell me; an address, perhaps, or a telephone number. I come to see you and find you are telephoning. But you know no one in Berlin to telephone. I do not think you have been very fair with me."

"Jesus! Fair with *you* . . . you—" And then he stopped. He had been about to tell her his own suspicions: of her pretence at journalism; of her lying. But he was cautious now. After a while she left and he did not try to stop her.

\*     \*     \*

The Europa Centre, where Spencer had had coffee the first morning, is a huge complex of offices, shops and a hotel at the apex of a triangle formed by Budapesterstrasse, Tauentzien-strasse and the Breitscheidplatz, and only about seven minutes' walk from his hotel. The single tower of the hotel rises from the complex, as a factory chimney rises from its buildings. The shopping plaza is on several floors, a place of dark, reflective surfaces, potted trees, courts, escalators, benches and winding glass alleys. At its centre is a square ice-rink. There are shops on each floor, boutiques, men's shops, photo-graphic, stereo, print, jeans, a joke shop, others selling porce-lain, books, leatherware and handbags, pastries, gifts; there are restaurants and coffee shops, bars and a bank. There are also half a dozen entrances and exits.

Spencer left the bitterly cold and misty air of Tauentzien-strasse and entered the Centre's warm, dim world. To his right, behind glass windows and doors, was the ice-rink, but he was early, and like some subconsciously wary animal he went up on the escalator to a viewing gallery from where he could look down on the skaters. He studied the wide corridor surrounding the rink but there were few spectators and he could not recognize anyone resembling Willi. He spent ten minutes moving round the upstairs balcony slowly enough to give himself a good view of everyone below.

He inspected the skaters. They consisted of two elderly couples, skating carefully to a Viennese waltz. The women, old as they were, wore leotards over their thick and varicosed legs; the men, plus-fours and *loden* jackets. At first they seemed to him farcical as they slid around the ice with their stiff, cautious movements. But they were unaware that some of the spectators were watching them with amusement, instead they gripped each other like young lovers, and waltzed in an enclosed dreamworld, oblivious of anyone. They looked like the couples who had been there on his previous visit and he wondered if they came every day.

He wandered through the plaza, stopping every now and then, going into shops, using the abundant plate glass as a mirror. He came down to the ground floor and was looking into the window of a glass shop when he saw something shadowy behind him. He moved to get a better view and had the briefest glimpse of a portly man in a coat with a turned-up collar carrying a square white patisserie box. He turned but the figure had vanished. He went along the glass-sided alley and saw the man rising to the first floor on the escalator. His image-filled mind registered the figure with a feeling of shock. There was something about him . . . Was he Bruno?

He crossed to the escalator and followed. But as he rose he glanced at the down escalator. The man was sinking to the ground floor. Spencer could not see his face.

He paused on the first floor trying to decide what to do. Then he followed the man on down the escalator.

On the ground floor again he looked through the glass windows onto the ice-rink, but the man was not there, nor was he anywhere in sight. There was another escalator to the

166

basement and Spencer stepped onto this. He searched through the shops, but there was no sign of the man. He moved to a shop with a rack of prints outside it and pretended to study them while watching the escalator. A print caught his eye. In the few seconds he looked away the man carrying the patisserie box had stepped onto the escalator and, when he turned back, was already half way up to the ground floor.

Spencer hurried after him. He watched the figure cross the court with the potted shrubs and go into another shopping alley. He was about to follow when he saw a flash of blue. He glanced to his right just as a blue suede coat disappeared round a corner on the far side of the plaza. He was about to see if it belonged to Lilo when he brought himself up short. It was ridiculous. He would be seeing Campbell next. He looked at his watch and went through the doors to the ice-rink. The doors opened onto a wide corridor running around the four sides, separated from the ice by a wall low enough to lean on. Pillars every few metres supported the gallery above. ⁓

He walked around the ice-rink looking for Willi. He was nowhere to be seen. He stopped by a pillar to wait. There was something not quite right about the atmosphere. Every nerve in Spencer's body was telling him to leave. He decided to wait only five minutes.

"Hello, Johnnie," a voice said at his elbow. Spencer whipped round. He was looking at a portly man with a fleshy, pink face that shone with good living. It was Bruno. He had gone bald except for a tonsure of light gingerish hair, and there were freckles on his scalp. He was wearing a black leather coat with a fur collar and holding a pair of light yellow pigskin gloves in one hand. In the other he carried a patisserie box. He was the man Spencer had seen on the escalator. Altogether he looked sleek, well-fed and prosperous. In his eyes was that same calculating look that Spencer remembered. The last time he had seen it was in the cellar after the bombing.

Bruno put down the box on the wall next to the pillar and held out his hand. Spencer found himself gripping it before he could react. "It's nice to see you again," Bruno said. "Is this your first visit to Berlin since the war?"

167

It was said blandly as though the only thing between them was a slight acquaintanceship.

"Yes," he said, trying to get a grip on himself.

"It's changed, no? I mean, we did not have all this in those days." He waved a large well-manicured hand around him. "Then this was just rubble. Do you remember we used to walk past it sometimes on our way home from a meeting?"

"How did you know I was here?" Spencer said, but Bruno ignored the question.

"I often think of those days. I wouldn't like to go back to them, but they weren't so bad in some ways. There was a comradeship among Berliners that no longer exists. I mean, you remember that, don't you, Johnnie? You'd do anything for a friend then, no thought of rewards." He looked at his watch and then at the two elderly couples moving round the rink to the taped music.

"They say war brings out the worst and the best in people. Don't you agree, Johnnie? It was a struggle, but it was a struggle for everyone. Just because you had money you couldn't buy yourself a safe place. I think it wasn't such a materialistic society, if you know what I mean. It was share and share alike. If one person had a bottle of schnapps he shared it with his friends, he didn't try to hide it." Spencer thought of the shoe-boxes filled with loot under the wardrobe. "Now everyone drives in his own Mercedes and all he wants is a better hi-fi set or a more expensive camera." He shook his head sadly. "No, in some ways the old days were better."

Spencer was only half listening to this fulsome nonsense, the other part of his mind was considering his own position. How did Bruno know he'd be here? What did he want? Where had he come from? It was Willi of course. Willi had wanted to play his own game; the archetypal middle man. Clearly he had laid this whole thing on but if he'd known where Bruno was in the beginning why hadn't he sold the information to Spencer?

"You remember the house in Graf Speestrasse," Bruno was saying. "You remember how friendly we were there. How my mother used to work miracles with the food ration. Remember Herr Lange? He married my mother you know. They were a

168

great comfort to each other, especially in her last days. Yes . . .
we lived for each other then . . . but now!"

Listening to him Spencer felt he was beginning to lose his
grip on reality and he decided to play Bruno's game; at least
for the moment; pretending there was nothing in the background at all except anodyne memories; churning out plati-
tudes; little pleasantries. "You've done well," he said,
businessman talking to businessman.

"So, so. There were opportunities after the war, Johnnie.
I mean, for people with a little brain."

"And a little money."

"Of course. I wish you had stayed. We'd have done well,
you and I. Comrades in war and peace." He glanced at his
watch. "You know when I went to school there was a stained
glass window showing a dying soldier from the First War—"

"Yes, you told me about the window."

"Well, that's what I mean. We could have done great things.
I looked for you. Searched all over town but you were nowhere
to be found." Spencer knew then that Bruno had gone back to
the cellar to make sure. What would have happened if he'd
found him there? A lump of concrete on the head? "And you
Johnnie. You've done well too. I sometimes saw your picture
in the financial papers. The John Spencer Group of Companies.
Very fine." He paused, looked at his watch again and said,
"Are you here on business?" It was a loaded, calculated
question.

"You know why I'm here," Spencer said.

"Expansion?"

"You say you read the papers."

"Of course. I like to keep abreast of things."

"Then you read of the shooting in London in which my wife
was killed."

"That's so, Johnnie, but I didn't like to bring it up."

"Naturally."

"Tragic. So young too."

"Yes. Young and beautiful and pregnant."

"It's really dreadful what happens these days. That's what
I was saying, Johnnie. The war was better. More comradeship.

One knew the reason for things then. One was fighting for one's life." He glanced at his watch again and Spencer felt the anger rising inside him. He fought against it. He knew the only way to conduct the present discussion was to follow Bruno's lead. To keep it cool; always cool.

"I've been telephoning you for two days," Spencer said.

"I've been away."

"On business?"

"Yes."

"What is your business, Bruno?"

"A little of this, a little of that. Import. Export. You know how it is." He looked at his watch again.

"Are you in a hurry?"

"I have another appointment. Please tell me what you wish."

"You must have some idea."

"Why should I? You are being very mysterious, Johnnie. I thought it was two old friends meeting after a long time."

Spencer was suddenly angry. "Don't talk balls. You know as well as I do what I want."

"Perhaps it is something you cannot have."

"Listen to me, Bruno, the police know about you."

Bruno shrugged. "What can they know?"

"They have a photograph."

Bruno swung round to face him. "You're lying!"

"They showed it to me in London."

"Who?"

"A Chief Superintendent."

"What was his name?"

"Hoest."

Bruno began fiddling with his watch. Now, as the name was spoken, he made a sound like a sigh, a slight explosive exhalation.

He looked at the time again, then said, "I must get some cigarettes. I will be back in a minute."

He hurried through the glass doors. It was odd, Spencer thought, he had never smoked before. He had often criticized Lange for his excessive use of cigarettes; so he had finally

170

succumbed himself. Spencer glanced at the skaters. There was only one couple now, the older of the two. The man had his right arm behind the woman, gripping her right arm at the elbow. Their left hands were clasped. They danced as though they were the only two people in the world.

He looked up at the gallery. Lilo was standing there looking at him. His first reaction was one of shock then outrage then, when he saw the gun gleaming in her hand, fear. He sprang behind the pillar then swung from side to side like a hunted animal. He could see through the glass doors into the leather-ware shop beyond. Bruno was standing in the shop. He was behind a rack of handbags but for one brief instant Spencer saw his face. He was staring back through the glass doors as though waiting for something. The loudspeakers were playing Waldteufel. The old couple were gliding around the ice. Spencer saw everything as though in slow motion. He knew he had to get out of there. His legs began to churn slowly as though he were running in deep sand. He had not gone more than a few steps when the bomb in the patisserie box exploded.

He felt the shock wave hit him, lift him and fling him across the corridor. He saw glass windows and doors buckle and disintegrate. He seemed to hear a continuous screeching noise and then he crashed into the far wall and fell.

The screeching continued, refining itself, until he could separate it into its components. They were individual human screams. He got to his knees and then his feet. Glass was everywhere. It crunched under his shoes.

The patisserie box had been placed next to the pillar and it had been Spencer's movement, after he had seen Bruno, that had saved him. The pillar had shielded him, but great lumps of concrete had been blown out of it.

People seemed to be running towards him across the ice and around the corridor; some were trying to escape, others were running towards something on the ice he could not see. He tottered to the low wall and what he saw brought the bile up into his throat. The old skating couple must have been exactly opposite the bomb when it went off. The ice was drenched with blood. What looked like parts of a human arm

171

lay some metres away. The bodies were intertwined as they had been in life but now they made up a mangled heap of flesh. Some people were trying to separate them; a woman was crying; half a dozen onlookers stood staring down in morbid fascination.

Spencer's terror was replaced by a violent anger. He turned to where he had last seen Bruno. The glass doors between the ice-rink and the shopping precinct were smashed to pieces; so were several shops, including the one that sold leatherware. The rack of handbags lay on the floor. A woman was dabbing at a red rivulet on her forehead. Bruno was nowhere to be seen. He glanced up at the gallery; Lilo too was gone.

He ran out of the ice-rink into the shopping precinct. The place was in uproar. Shops along one alley had been damaged. There was glass everywhere. People had been cut. Others, like himself, were running towards the exits. He joined a throng and within seconds found himself out in Budapesterstrasse. He heard the sound of police sirens from the direction of the Kurfurstendamm. He ran a few metres to his right and then began to walk. Soon he was enveloped by the mist and within several minutes was entering the door of his hotel.

He went up to his room and was sick into the lavatory. He rinsed his mouth then poured himself a stiff whisky. He sat on the bed. All his limbs were trembling and when he raised the glass to his mouth he had to hold it with both hands. He could not erase the picture of the two old people dead on the ice; their blood mixing with the slush. And he knew it was his fault, just as Sue's death had been his fault. Perhaps there was little he could have done about Sue, but if he had gone to the police about Bruno as he should have done they might have caught him now, or even if they hadn't he would have been on the run and the two old people would still be waltzing round and round to the music of Waldteufel. But he had been stopped by the thought of what the revelation would do to his life; it was not the way of a survivor.

For most of his adult life he had rationalized the act of joining the British Free Corps by telling himself that he had been only sixteen, that he hardly knew what being a traitor

172

was, and that in any case he had been a totally different person, a stranger almost. Now came the terrible thought that the child really was the father of the man, that the flaw in his psyche that had made itself evident then had never been repaired; that, if anything, the lesion might have grown worse.

He came back to the red stain on the ice and the heaps of flesh. He saw again the bodies of Tellier and Susan by the front door of his Hampstead house, the body of Frau Mentzel, half buried in the rubble of the cellar, her head stove in by the lump of concrete. And all killed by Bruno. What was it Hoest had said in London? Five dead in a store in Cologne, three dead in Hanover, two dead in bank robberies. He was like some primitive barbarian, a Visigoth or a Hun, leaving a trail of blood wherever he went.

Spencer knew that if he did not do something now he never would. He picked up the telephone and asked to be put through to the police. He spoke to the central switchboard and asked for Hoest in a mixture of German and English. The officer could speak a little English and he said he would put him through to the Kriminalpolizei. But then he was connected with a man who had no English at all and in his distress Spencer's own German deserted him. He was speaking too fast and stumbling over his words; thinking in English and trying to translate directly into German. The man hardly understood a word. Finally he asked Spencer to hold on. The shake in Spencer's hands became worse under the stress of telephoning. The man's voice returned. He spoke slowly in German and explained that Hoest was not available. What was it that the Herr wanted? Spencer opened his mouth, but closed it again, daunted by the overwhelming task of trying to explain. Instead he simply replaced the receiver. He sat there with the sweat drying on him, still shaking with reaction. Then he got to his feet and took his gun from his suitcase and checked the magazine. It was ironic that now he wanted to hand over his responsibility Hoest was not there to take it; he was forced to go on by himself. And he had to act quickly or Bruno would be lost again in a world of safe-houses. He must get the address from Willi even if he had to beat it out of him.

There were no taxis to be seen in Kurfurstenstrasse and so he began to hurry in the direction of Willi's house. He could not shake off the pictures in his mind of the dead ice skaters. And again he saw Lilo standing in the gallery above, the gun in her hand. Why hadn't she killed him earlier, she had had plenty of opportunity? How did a woman with a son like Peter live such a Jekyll and Hyde existence? That's what he couldn't grasp. He was right to have been suspicious of her from the beginning. What had she been doing there? Was she Bruno's bodyguard? His mistress? Was Bruno the father of the child? That hardly seemed likely. And he'd been drawn to her. That's what made him feel sick. After what had happened to Sue, he had gone to bed with her. Lilo, a terrorist, a criminal, someone who used sex simply as part of her business.

He hurried on through the misty streets, filled with anger and self-disgust. But he could atone. That was one thing he held onto.

The house, when he reached it in the wilderness of brown grass and dirty snow, was curtained against the day. He went down the basement steps and rang the bell. He heard it ringing inside. No one came. He rang again. Then he banged on the door with his hand. It swung slowly open. The room was in darkness and he closed the door behind him and switched on the light. The first thing he saw was the old woman asleep in her wheel-chair and then, as he moved farther into the room, he noticed the papers strewn on the floor. It looked as though someone had deliberately flung them there. "Excuse me," he said. She didn't move. "Excuse me," he said again, and shook her shoulder gently. The pressure caused the chair to move. The floor itself must have been sloping, probably from the bombing, because the chair ran slowly backwards the width of the room until it came to rest under the shelves where she kept her press-cutting books. The shelves were empty now. As the chair bumped to a stop her head lolled forward and she slipped gently onto the carpet. Horrified, Spencer went forward to lift her back again, and saw the marks on her neck. She was cold to the touch and someone had strangled her. The pressure had been so great that blood had risen to the surface where the fingertips had been. He started back and looked wildly round the room. He was on the point of leaving when he remembered his pistol, and took it from the jacket pocket. It gave him comfort.

Had Willi done this, he wondered? Had he finally decided to end the association with his grandmother? He opened the living-room door and went into a passage beyond. From it he could look into what appeared to be a bedroom. The light was on and he could see a pair of feet extending beyond the bottom of the bed. Cautiously he looked around the door. It was Willi. He was tied to the bed. Spencer saw his right hand first, blackened with sulphurous yellow lines on the fingers and knew what he would find on the floor. It was there: the toaster. Willi, too, had been strangled; he, too, was cold. It didn't take Spencer long to work out what must have happened. Willi had tried to play an adult game. He must have found Bruno's trail, starting with the press cuttings and going on from there. He had probably tried to squeeze him for money in his role of middle man. He had sold Spencer the information about Bruno's wife; it didn't take much stretch of the imagination to see him trying to sell Bruno the information that someone called John Spencer was looking for him.

They had come here—probably the big, bearded man called Muller and the woman, Inge—and they had used the same persuasion on Willi as they had on Riemeck. So instead of Willi coming to the Europa Centre it had been Bruno with his patisserie box. He had set the timing adjustment to the bomb just before he had approached Spencer at the ice rink. That was why he had looked at his watch so often.

As these thoughts were crowding into Spencer's mind others were pressing him to do something. To get out. Anything, as long as it was action, movement. There was nothing he could do here for either Willi or his grandmother. He went from the bedroom and through the living-room and let himself out of the house.

He went up the basement steps and saw the little blue Beetle at the end of the road. His heart gave a sudden lurch until he realized that the man and woman in the front were the lunch-time lovers he had seen when he and Lilo had come to the house.

It had begun to snow and he bent his head into the small flakes and hurried back to the hotel. The reaction, the shaking and the trembling, the feeling of nausea which had come after the bomb blast in the Europa Centre did not return now. He felt calm, almost icily cold. He knew what he had to do, but the question was how? After what had happened in the Europa Centre Bruno would go to ground and Spencer would have no hope of finding him.

At the hotel he stopped at the telephonist's little cubby hole but she wasn't there. One of the porters was on duty while she had her lunch.

"I have a telephone number," he said. "Can you get me the address from it?"

"I do not think that is possible. For an address you must have the name."

"Would you try? I'll make it worth your while."

He shrugged. "If you wish." He dialled and talked rapidly in German and then put his hand over the harness mouthpiece. "It is as I said. For an address you must have a name."

He was looking up at Spencer expectantly and the lights on the board were flicking on and off, indicating that other people were wanting his attention.

A feeling of hopelessness swept over Spencer. "You could try . . ." He was about to say Riesenfeld, for it was the only other name he knew, when his subconscious produced another. Bruno had used it the very first day Spencer had come to Berlin from Bremerhaven. In those first few hours, when he had been excited about Spencer's arrival, he had told him how his father had been a member of the British Union of Fascists. Spencer could hear the echo of his voice in his mind. He could even see him pointing to the picture of his father in the upstairs bedroom, the father whose name was Lionel Boyse. "Boyse," Bruno had said. "That's my real name."

"Try the name Boyse." Spencer said feeling a cold flash of excitement. "B-o-y-s-e."

The porter spoke again and then he took up a pencil and

began to write on a pad. Spencer felt his heart racing. The porter tore off the page and handed it to him. He had difficulty in making out the spiky German writing. He could understand the words "Rattenburg Haus" but that was all. He turned back to the porter for amplification but he was already caught up with the next caller.

He took the tearsheet to the receptionist. "That is out of town," she said. "Near Wannsee."

"I don't know Berlin."

She picked up a folding map from the counter and opened it. "Here. This is the area." She pointed to a large body of water. "It is here, on this shore."

"How do I get there?"

"You can either go by car, park it and then walk through the forest, or you can drive to Wannsee and take a ferry to Moorlake and walk back along the shore a little. It would not be too far. If you do not have a car there is a Number 66 bus that leaves from the Zoo Station."

"What about a taxi?"

"It will be expensive."

He took a taxi.

Wannsee was a lakeside resort less than half an hour's drive westward from the centre. It was, he discovered, an arm of a much larger body of water called the Havel, which in turn was fed by the River Havel. In spite of yacht clubs and marinas and bathing areas, it had preserved a rural aspect. Much of the Havel's eastern shore was bordered by a thick forest of hardwoods, the Berlin Forest, which appeared to be an ideal place for naturalists and walkers. Spencer reached Wannsee well before noon. The lake was dead calm and mist hung over the shoreline. He paid off the taxi at the little harbour where the ferries tied up and took out the address and his map. The receptionist had marked an area of the lake-shore west of Wannsee near the tip of Peacock Island.

He went down to the harbour and bought a ticket for a boat leaving in ten minutes. It reminded him of the ones that took summer tourists up and down the Thames. There were rows of seats on the deck and more in a main cabin. He went into the warmth of the cabin. There were no tourists and few other passengers. They stopped first at the village of Kladow then swung south-west and sailed along the channel formed by Peacock Island and the shore of the lake. The shore was heavily bushed with massive trees coming down to the water's edge. Tall brown reeds, thick in places, rose to meet them. Everything was very still.

Dotted sparsely amid the dense growth he saw an occasional isolated house. They were huge country villas built probably at the turn of the century in every architectural style, some like small French chateaux, some in Black Forest Gothic, some Scottish baronial. All were large, exclusively set in their own patches of forest and cut off from their neighbours by wide belts of trees.

On the starboard side he could see the Berlin Wall. It swept down to the opposite shore at right angles and then turned and followed the water's edge. Made of grey concrete slabs with watch towers rising at intervals, it looked more out of place in this rural setting than it had among the dismal buildings of Checkpoint Charlie. As they came down the narrow body of water that was all that separated West from East, he could see the East German guard in the tower watching the boat through his binoculars.

They were going slowly as they came towards their final stop. On the West side of the lake signs in red and black had been placed at the water's edge. One read: ENDE DES AMERIKANISCHEN SEKTORS, then there was an arrow, and the words, NACH RE 70 METERN. Other signs warned visitors that the American sector extended only fifty or sixty metres into the centre of the channel. Beyond that was East Germany. On their side a West German police launch, the *Biber*, was cruising slowly up and down. Near the far bank a grey launch filled with grey-uniformed East German border guards, was keeping station with her.

The ferry approached a small wooden jetty. Beyond it he saw a notice which said in three languages: "Restricted area. Do not pass beyond this point. Reverse your course."

He was the only passenger to disembark. There was no one

178

on the jetty, no building in sight; he might have been a hundred miles from anywhere. As instructed, the boat reversed its course and turned again into the channel. The West German police launch suddenly opened its throttles and raced away towards Wannsee throwing up a creamy bow wave. The East German boat turned and went down the lake. He felt deserted.

He looked at the map again, took a path to the left and was immediately swallowed up by the forest. He walked for ten or twelve minutes parallel with the shore-line, then the path turned away towards the heart of the forest. He was under a canopy of bare branches and there was a smell of leaf-mould in the air. He came to another path branching away to the left. He stopped and considered. The only houses he had seen were by the water. That was the way the new path led. He turned down it.

This was much narrower. In about two hundred metres he came to a high barbed-wire fence. The path ran along it past a big, spiked wrought-iron gate of the sort that usually opens onto a carriage drive. But here it opened onto nothing at all. It was heavily padlocked with an old, discoloured chain. Leaves had blown against the bottom and lay in piles on either side. Spencer thought it had not been opened for years. Worked into the wrought-iron, so that it was part of the gate itself, were the words "Rattenburg Haus". He shivered in the cold. This was a setting for nightmares: a gate that did not open, a path that led nowhere. He could feel his heart thumping in his chest and he began to wonder whether he was not being a fool. But he thought of Sue's body lying by the front door of their house, and he thought of Bruno in the cellar of the bombed house, of the couple on the ice, of Willi on the bed, of the old woman. Thinking helped because it make him angry again and anger masked his fear. He touched the gun in his pocket and that, too, helped.

He went on past the gate for about another hundred metres before the fence turned down towards the water. There was no other entrance. Then, as he came past a thick screen of wild willow, he saw that a dead tree had been blown down in a recent gale. It had smashed onto the fence, bridging it. He stood for a few moments, listening and looking, but the forest was still. He climbed along the tree. It was a large beech and it was easy to cross. He stepped down onto a thick layer of leaves that made a swishing noise as he walked. Almost immediately he came to the back of the house. It was big and square and painted in that dark yellow which the Austrians call *kaisergelb*. He stood behind a tree and watched. Everything seemed to be closed up. He circled it and stood in a patch of reeds by the water's edge looking at the façade. The architect had given the house a classical pediment and he recalled noticing it as he had come past in the boat. It was heavily screened by trees on both sides and at the rear, and thick beds of reeds lay in front of it. Again he paused, but there was no movement. It seemed to be completely uninhabited.

A large flight of steps ran up to the terrace that stretched along the front. It was cracked in many places and weeds were spreading across it like a carpet. Several tables and chairs stood on the terrace but, like the gates, they were of wrought-iron and it was impossible to say if they had been used recently or ten years before.

The ground floor windows were covered from the inside by wooden shutters so, screened by trees, he made his way to the back of the house, but it was impossible to see through the windows there either, for those in which the glass was not frosted had net curtains hanging on the inside.

Something nagged at him, making him feel additionally uneasy. There was something not quite right about the house and its grounds. It wasn't that it seemed to exist in a decaying wilderness, but something more prosaic, more functional. It lacked any form of entrance. How, if people lived there, did they come and go? The great padlocked gate at the back did not open onto any roadway. As far as he could tell the fence was otherwise unbroken in its length around the house. They could not troop in and out through the forest. There had to be another way.

He withdrew again into the cover of the forest and let his eyes rove over the wild garden and the shuttered rooms. He

180

could see no evidence of human habitation. He turned and walked back towards the lakeshore. Here the reeds were heavy, tall and thick and in some places well over his head. The trees, too, crowded down to the water line. He found difficulty in seeing where land ended and water began, and it was only when his feet grew wet that he knew he had arrived at the lake itself. He moved through the reed-bed, parallel to the front of the house, trying to keep on dry land. The reeds clattered round him as he moved, and bits of their furry plumes fell on his head. He had not gone more than thirty or forty metres when they suddenly ended and he found himself looking at a channel cut through them, twisting and turning until it reached open water.

He broke off a reed and pushed it down but the water was too deep for him to touch bottom. He moved along the bank of the channel and came upon the low-hanging branches of a massive tree. He picked his way under them and on the far side found himself in a kind of enclosure. There were trees all around him, and at his back the channel and the reeds. In the midst of the enclosure was a boathouse. It was a substantial building and meant to take a large boat or several small ones. Again he stopped and watched it, but the big doors facing the lake were open and the slipway was empty.

In front of it, the channel had been widened and a red mooring buoy bobbed in the water. It was a big enough basin for a fair-sized craft to turn in. When he had satisfied himself that the boathouse was as devoid of human inhabitants as the house itself, he moved quietly through the reeds towards it and went into its cavernous interior. Along one of the walls were projecting brackets where rowing shells must once have been stored, one above the other. Now only one rotting canoe hung there. Above the canoe were wooden plaques, some with names, some with heraldic devices, but all so old and weathered and cracked that they were illegible and he assumed that they must have been sculling prizes won in the twenties or even before.

At the rear of the boathouse was a door. He tried it and it opened into a room built to hold oars and sails and ropes but

181

whose shelves were now empty. It was windowless and dark and some moments passed before he made out another door on the far side and crossed towards it. He saw something in front of the door which stopped him dead.

On the floor were two large cardboard boxes and in them were packets of cereal, cartons of milk, coffee, bread and sugar, butter, smoked sausage. There were tins, packets of soup, lavatory paper, kitchen paper, eggs, and on top of one was an itemized list. What he was looking at was a delivery of groceries. Next to the boxes were gas cylinders of the sort used for coupling up to a cooker. Someone had phoned and ordered the groceries, which meant that someone was expected at the house.

But was that someone Bruno? He might be anywhere. The house might belong to someone else by now. Why, he wondered, had the groceries been placed where they were, in front of the second door? What lay on the far side? Was it another part of the boathouse where there were living quarters? Was that why the main house seemed so derelict? He tried the door but it was locked. He ran his fingers along the lintel hoping to find a key, but all he found was dust. Yet, he reasoned, there must be a key nearby, if the owner of the house was like most other people. His own experience told him that you did not only carry a key, you hid one near the door in case you lost or forgot the key you were carrying. He began to search the room. Every few moments he paused and listened for the sound of a launch but there was only the stillness of the misty lake.

It took him fifteen minutes to find the key. It had been taped to the bottom of the lowest shelf. He pulled it off and unlocked the door. He found himself looking into a passage-way, and switched on the light. The passage rose in a gentle gradient and he could not see the far end because there was a bend in the middle. Then he noticed that it had no windows. It wasn't a passage, then, but a tunnel.

He paused. If he went on now his actions might be irrevo-cable. It was one thing, in the hot black aftermath of Sue's death to decide to find Bruno and to take his vengeance. It was another to enter the lair. He had seen what Bruno could do both when he was a youth and now as an adult. He wasn't equipped to deal with him. He needed Hoest; needed to be able to hand over what he'd found. But what had he found and could he be sure? *Did* Bruno live here? He thought of the groceries behind him. Clearly there was no one in the house. Perhaps they had left already. Perhaps they were even now in some other safe-house in another part of Berlin and the groceries would rot here until Doomsday. There was only one way to find out and he owed that to Sue and to the dead couple on the ice and to Willi and to Willi's grandmother and to old Mrs Mentzel whose husband brought a nice piece of cheese home on a Saturday night. And the more he thought of Hoest and his silly hat and his baggy eyes and his windy stomach the less faith he had in him. Spencer made his decision.

He closed the door behind him but did not lock it, and began to walk slowly along the tunnel. When he rounded the bend he could see another door at the far end and he estimated that the tunnel was about forty metres long. It was carpeted, with matting, so his feet made little noise. He paused at the other end, straining to hear any sound from the far side. But as before, everything was still.

He opened the door and went into the house. What little light entered through cracks in the wooden shutters showed him he was standing in the entrance hall. He knew then that the tunnel leading from the boathouse to the main house was, in effect, its front door. Why it had originally been built this way he could not imagine. Perhaps the owner had wished to smuggle in his mistresses unobserved, or perhaps it was an easy, if expensive, way of reaching the house without being rained on. It was perfect for someone like Bruno.

The hall was formal and neat. There was a large carved chest, a table, a wall mirror, a vase containing dried flowers.

He tip-toed across and went into the drawing-room. Modern chairs, two sofas, a Breughel print, fire-place, a magazine rack without magazines, a reproduction Louis Quinze writing-table. Newspapers were thrown down and there was a drinks table on which stood a bottle of *tafelwein* half empty. He silently checked the rooms downstairs, a dining-room, a study, a kitchen. There was the remains of a meal on the kitchen table. It looked as though the inhabitants had left in a hurry. He looked for something that would give identity to the occupants but the kitchen contained no secrets. All was white vitreous enamel and white-painted wood. Why was the inside so neat and modern, so well-kept, and the outside allowed to fall into ruin and decay?

He went carefully up the stairs. Bedrooms led off the upstairs hall. One bedroom was unused but a second had a big double bed. Clothes, male and female, were flung on the floor. Muller and Inge? He moved on down the hall until he came to the last bedroom, and this was different. The room was feminine: full of soft pinks and pastel shades, a four-poster with hangings, white goatskin rugs on the floor, an inlaid dressing table with split mirrors. On the far side of the bed and flush with the wall so that it looked almost part of the moulding pattern, was the door of a hanging cupboard. Spencer opened it. A light, controlled by the door, came on.

It was a big walk-in cupboard and several suits and coats were hanging on the rail. On a shelf above the rail were cardboard boxes which had once held new clothing. He felt in the pockets of a dark blue suit. Nothing. He looked inside the jacket. There was no maker's label or shop label. He looked at the suit next to it. Once again the pockets were empty and the labels gone. He went along the rack. Each suit, each jacket was exactly the same. Finally he came to a field-grey jacket of military cut. He paused. It held no clue as to ownership, nor even to origin. Then his eye caught something. It was the collar. There was an area that seemed slightly darker than the rest. He looked more closely. Near the other collar point he saw the same dark area. He took the jacket off its hanger and carried it to the light. Now he could just make out the faint marks of the stitches. Someone had carefully removed emblems, or patches from both sides of the collar. One of those patches had come to him in an envelope in London. The other had been found by German police in a stolen Volkswagen microbus discovered on the Portsmouth road. They were the collar patches showing heraldic leopards, the patches worn by members of the British Free Corps. He was in Bruno's bedroom.

Just then he heard the noise of a match being struck somewhere nearby. The cupboard door was almost closed. Then he remembered the light. A voice said:

"Is that you, John Spencer? Knock once for yes, twice for no."

He froze.

"Come out, dear," the voice said. "Come out and let's have a look at you."

The door was pulled open and a young woman stood on the threshold. She was pretty in a rather coarse way with a thin face and hair cut like a boy's. She wore a long kaftan in sludgy greens and browns, heavy green eye-shadow, drop ear-rings and several large rings of rose quartz and malachite on her fingers. She was lighting a cigarette in a holder.

"Don't be surprised," she said. "I've been watching you from the window."

"How did you know it was me?"

"I said to myself, 'I wonder who that is?'" She spoke in a low voice, somewhat husky, with a marked cockney accent. "Who'd be paying us a visit at this time of day. The police? But then I looked out the other windows and there was no one. And we don't have friends to lunch. Especially friends that come over the fence with bang-bangs. So I thought, 'Who's been a clever boy, then? Who's tracked Bruno down?'"

"He tried to kill me."

"You got in his way, dear. He kills everybody who gets in his way. He's very *violent* is Bruno. Not to look at. But you know what I mean."

She went backwards into the room and he followed her. "He planted a bomb," he said. "It was meant for me. Instead it killed two old people."

She made a sound with her lips. "I keep on telling him. I say, 'Bruno, that's not the way to do business.' It's so unnecessary. Never mind the *noise*." She looked him over, then said, "I'll say one thing for Bruno. He could always pick 'em."

"What's that supposed to mean?"

"Anyone can see you must have been a pretty boy. I prefer older men, see? More mature, like . . ."

"Where are they?" Spencer said.

"Who?"

"You know damn well who."

"Temper. You mean Bruno and Jurgen? They'll be back. Don't worry."

"Where's the woman who was at my house in London?"

"Inge? She's with the boat. You'll see her, too. You'll see everyone. We'll have a party." She turned away from him. "Well, I can't stay chatting. I suppose we'll be leaving once they get back. Such a pity about the house. We'll never find another one like it. One of Bruno's friends let us have it a couple of years ago. Such a nice man. A lawyer, I think he is. Do you mind if I pack?" She had opened the door of the hanging cupboard and was reaching up for a suitcase.

"Forget it," Spencer said. "There'll be no need for that."

"Now I suppose we'll have to find another one. But Bruno's got lots of friends."

"I said, leave it!"

She had gripped the small suitcase with her hand and now she turned and threw it at him. One of its corners caught him high up on the cheek, knocking him onto the bed. She was on him in a flash. He found himself enveloped in the kaftan like a leopard in a net. She was incredibly fast and had a body like whipcord. They rolled off the bed onto the floor. She was trying to get the gun and Spencer needed all his strength to hold onto it. He felt her teeth sink into his wrist and he brought up his knee into her stomach. She coughed and momentarily released her hold. He tried to club her with the gun but again she was onto him like a wild animal, all arms and legs.

Somehow she had managed to get her legs around his throat and was able to use both hands to try and get the gun. She began to bang his hand against the leg of the bed. She caught his thumb and bent it backwards. The agony was too much for him. He opened his hand and the gun flew across the floor. She went after it but he caught at the kaftan. It ripped. She got to her feet and he saw the back of her naked body as she sprang for the gun. One foot was in the folds of the kaftan. She tripped and fell forward. There was a crash of glass as her head went through the window. She tried to scream but all he could hear was a gurgling noise. He picked himself up and crossed to her. Blood was pouring down her neck and the window frame. He lifted her off the window. The glass had cut her throat. He saw what he had not seen before. She wasn't a girl, but a young man. Spencer brought him back into the room and laid him on the carpet. He was bubbling and gasping and Spencer watched him in a daze. He was weak, drained, numb. He crouched, staring at the young man, unable to take in what was happening.

There was a noise behind him and people came into the room. He heard Bruno's voice: "Oh, Christ, he's killed Norman!" He felt a terrible blow on the side of his face and he fell onto the body. He knew another blow was coming and put up a hand to try to ward it off.

Instead, there was a noise from outside the house. A voice, magnified. "This is the police," it said in German. "The house is surrounded."

Someone switched out the light and Spencer could hear running feet. A few moments later a woman—Inge—said, "It's true!" Her voice was terrified. "They're all around. I can see them at the back."

Bruno said, "Go to the front room. See if they are down at the boathouse."

Spencer was left alone with Bruno and the dead body. "Get up!" Bruno said.

Spencer pulled himself up onto the bed. "Why?" Bruno said, kneeling by Norman's body and taking his head in his arms. "Why did you kill him? He did no harm." Spencer saw he was weeping.

The blow to his head and the sudden rise to his feet had made him feel giddy and sick. He was suffering from double vision. He sat, trying to collect his senses. Bruno was holding one of Norman's dead hands.

187

The big man in the white T-shirt, whom he now recognized as Jurgen Muller, came in. "They are just below the terrace. I can't see any near the boathouse."

At first, Bruno did not seem to hear. Then slowly he got to his feet. He bent and folded Norman's hands on his chest, then straightened. After a moment he said, "We'll use the tunnel."

"What about him?" Muller pointed to Spencer.

"Leave him to me."

They went downstairs. Muller and Inge led. Spencer and Bruno followed. Bruno had a heavy Walther PPK in his hand and he kept the barrel pressed at the nape of Spencer's neck. They went into the tunnel and waited for a minute. Then the voice came through the bull-horn again.

"The house is surrounded. You have five minutes to give yourselves up. In five minutes we will attack you."

The four went silently down the tunnel. The only light was the flame from Muller's cigarette lighter. At the far door Bruno said, "Let him go first in case there is shooting." He pushed Spencer forward. He would have fallen if Muller had not held him upright.

In a daze he opened the door. Grey daylight was seeping into the sailroom. No one was there. As they went from the sailroom to the slipway they could hear another announcement on the bull-horn.

In the turning basin below the boathouse, tied to the red buoy, was the boat they had arrived in while Spencer had been talking to Norman. It was a thirty-foot launch with a big Evinrude engine. Muller caught one of the ropes and pulled it towards a small jetty.

"Do we take him?" Inge whispered.

"Until we reach the car," Bruno said.

They got into the boat, Muller cast off and lowered the propeller into the water. He touched the engine covering. "She's still warm," he said.

Bruno and Inge crouched down, but Spencer collapsed onto the deck planking.

Muller started the engine. It fired first time with an enormous roar. He swung the boat into the channel that led to the lake. Then the mist was broken by an incandescent light. As they raced towards open water, they saw the police launch *Biber*. Its searchlight punched through the mist like a laser.

"Halt!" a voice shouted.

The cruiser was gaining momentum. There was a gap between the *Biber* and the reeds and Muller aimed her bow at it and at the same time he opened the throttle wide. The boat shot forward. Other lights appeared on the *Biber*'s deck. In the mist they looked like sparklets. Then there was firing. Muller took the first burst in the chest and fell over the engine. He grasped the tiller, trying to keep himself upright. The boat swung wildly, first one way, and then, as he struggled, the other. The bow ripped into the reeds and the boat was still. Water was pouring in where the hull had been holed.

Inge leapt ashore. The firing continued. She stumbled, crashing through the reeds. There was another burst. Pieces of splintered reeds shot up into the air as the bullets cut into the thick bed. She screamed and fell, got up, fell again, and then there was silence.

"Can you hear me?" Bruno shouted.

*"Ja."*

"I have the Englishman Spencer." He turned to Spencer. "Get up! Get up!" Spencer pulled himself to his feet and stood swaying. "If you shoot now," Bruno shouted, "you will kill him."

The boat was held by reeds and they were able to step ashore. The water was up to their knees. "Move!" Bruno said, encircling Spencer's neck with his left arm.

They went forward into the reed bed. The water that had seeped into his clothes when the boat was holed, and the shock of the cold water on his legs helped to revive him. They went through the reeds like Siamese twins, the umbilicus of Bruno's arm joining them.

Spencer could hear voices, some from where the *Biber* had been and others, obviously the police, coming down from the house to the water's edge. But they had moved some distance and the mist was thick. The police were making so much noise themselves that no one could hear them.

There was a shout of triumph well to their rear and Spencer thought they must have found Muller's body. They came to the tall barbed-wire fence that ran down into the water and turned inland to follow it, leaving the reeds behind. The underbrush was still thick and Spencer realized they were making for the fallen tree. If Bruno got over the fence into the forest the police would need dogs to find him, and he doubted they had brought dogs. Which meant that once over the fence Bruno might be safe, and once he felt safe Spencer knew that his own life would be over. He knew Bruno would not shoot him because the noise of the shot would reveal his presence. He would probably use the gun like a club and smash in his skull as he had smashed in the skull of Mrs Mentzel. Then anger returned, saving him from fear.

They came to the tree and he knew that this was where Bruno was going to kill him. They would have to clamber over separately. Bruno would have to release him. Looking at it from Bruno's viewpoint, anything could happen. Spencer might make a run for it; he, Bruno, might slip and the noise of the gun would be a liability. Spencer was facing the fallen tree when he felt the constriction of Bruno's arm slacken. He put his foot against the trunk and pushed as hard as he could. His body flew back into Bruno's, knocking him to the ground.

"Here!" Spencer shouted. "Here! Over here!"

He began to run, still shouting. Bruno fired from less than thirty feet. The heavy bullet caught Spencer in the left shoulder, spinning him round and knocking him to the ground.

Bruno fired again but Spencer had fallen among the trailing branches of the tree and the bullet was deflected. It was a big beech with a number of large branches, some of which had broken in the fall. Spencer pulled himself in, burrowing among them like a wounded animal. Bruno fired again. Bark flew from a branch in front of Spencer's face.

"Here!" he shouted again, "Here!"

He caught a glimpse of Bruno's face only feet away. He was

sweating, his eyes seemed mad. There was one major branch as thick as a man's waist behind which Spencer had taken refuge. Now, as Bruno moved towards him, he tried to penetrate even further among the branches, but they formed a lattice-work, a screen through which he could not push. He stared at Bruno, hypnotized by the effort it was costing the fat man. He was groaning and grunting and dragging himself along on his elbows, his need to kill Spencer overwhelming everything else.

Spencer searched desperately for something with which to defend himself. Suddenly it was like being in the cellar again after the bombing of Berlin. He could not move and the wolf was coming for him. His hand closed on a stone as it had closed then on a piece of rubble. Bruno had reached the large branch and was pulling himself into a kneeling position. He held the gun in both hands, resting it on a branch. Spencer was unable to draw back his arm far enough for a proper throw. He flicked the stone. It hit Bruno on the cheek, but not hard enough to injure. Bruno brushed at it with his hand then bent carefully to take aim again. There was something implacable, remorseless, in the way he slowly brought down the gun barrel. There was a noise behind him and, abruptly, he began to move backwards. Someone had grabbed him by the ankles and was pulling him bodily from the tree. There was a sound of threshing, of branches breaking and of blows, and then silence.

By the time they had helped Spencer out, Bruno was standing handcuffed to two policemen, his head bowed  blood dripping from the corner of his mouth.

There were eight or ten plain-clothes men, some with handguns and one or two with sub-machine guns. In the centre of the group Spencer recognized a Tyrolean hat with a large pheasant's feather on one side. Underneath it was the baggy-eyed face of Chief Superintendent Karl Hoest.

"Good day, Herr Spencer," he said, and then he saw the blood on Spencer's coat. "Is it bad?"

"I don't know. It's numb."

"Come, we must get you to a doctor."

He said something quickly in German and one of the officers took Spencer's right arm and they moved down towards the lake. He turned to look at Bruno but the fat man was staring down at the ground.

The *Biber* had come into the turning circle and was at the small jetty.

"How did you know?" Spencer said.

"About what?"

"All this."

Hoest smiled wearily. "You found out for us."

Hoest and Spencer and the officer helping Spencer led the little group down the slope. A plain-clothes man came running up, his trousers wet to the thighs. "We have found the woman," he said. "She's dead."

Hoest said, "That makes everybody."

As he said it a figure rose from the reeds in front of them. At first in the mist Spencer thought it was another plain-clothes policeman and then he saw it was Lilo. She was holding a gun in both hands and was aiming at his chest. He stopped. Terror gripped him. He opened his mouth to shout: "Why?" and then she fired.

He heard a cry behind him. He began to turn. As he did so one of the plain-clothes men returned the fire. Lilo seemed to jerk backwards as if on a string and lay on her back in the reeds. Bruno would also have fallen but he was held up by the handcuffs. She had shot him near the mouth and had blown away a portion of the back of his head.

\*       \*       \*

They were in an ambulance on the autobahn to Berlin. Lilo lay on the bunk on one side. A doctor was giving her blood. Hoest and Spencer sat on the opposite side near the rear doors. Spencer was still suffering from the blow to the head. "You *used* her," he said. It was the second time he had made the accusation.

"I won't deny it," Hoest said. "But she used us, too."

"You sent her to London. You sent her to meet me. All this shit about being a journalist—"

"That was true. She had been a journalist once."

"You knew she was with me all the time. You knew exactly what I was doing every minute." He thought of the lunch-time lovers in the Beetle. He thought of Lilo and himself in bed together. Had they known of that, too?

"That is what we hoped. But you did not co-operate with us and later she did not co-operate with us."

"So?"

"We followed you ourselves."

"You used me as the stalking horse. But it went wrong, didn't it?"

"Only when Lilo played her own game. I became suspicious. Right at the end. Yesterday. So we began to follow both of you."

Spencer recalled the telephone call in Lilo's apartment. It must have been one of Hoest's men checking on her.

Hoest nodded. "We know now she went to the hotel after you had left. The porter gave her the address he had found for you."

"I thought she was one of *them*," Spencer said, his mind still on the house.

"She didn't report in as we had planned," Hoest said. "Two or three times we had no idea where she was. That was when I began to have suspicions."

Lilo groaned and the doctor bent over her again. "I thought . . ." Spencer began, and then he paused. "I don't know what I thought."

"Did you think she liked you? More than that?"

"I had no right to."

"It's easy to make a mistake."

"It wasn't a mistake! You don't *know*. I went to her apartment. I saw her child. What will become of him?"

"Don't worry, we'll look after him. He's with his grandmother now."

"Peter," Spencer said. "That's his name. Peter."

"Yes," Hoest said wearily. "I know."

Suddenly Spencer said sharply, "How could you let her get involved in this?"

The doctor turned to them. "Please lower your voices!"

"Didn't I tell you?" Hoest said.

"Tell me what?"

"She came to *us*. I have known the family for years. I knew her father. She offered to help. That's why we sent her to London. It was *her* idea. We had a feeling even then that there were things you had not told us."

"But *why?* That's what I don't understand. Why?"

"She is Riemeck's widow."

"You mean the man—? That Riemeck!"

"That's right, Herr Spencer. The policeman who was tortured and killed in your house. And did she never tell you about her father?"

"A little. He was· used as a hostage in a terrorist raid. And then they shot him."

"That is correct. But after he was killed the authorities released a group of terrorists they had in gaol. So his life went for nothing, you see. No one was punished. Just the opposite; people were freed. It is understandable that when her husband was killed she said to herself, perhaps it may happen again. Perhaps no one will be punished. Or if they are punished, it will mean a few years in gaol and then some other terrorist will release them. It was better, you see, to have him dead. That way she could make sure. You must understand that. It is what you tried to do yourself. You and Lilo were after the same man. She knew it, you did not."

Spencer held his head in his hands and after a moment he said dully, "I thought I was using her. But she was using me— and you were using us both."

"Don't feel too badly. It worked. We have had a big success. The case is closed, yes?"

Was there something behind the words, did Hoest know about him? What, Spencer wondered, would have happened if Hoest had not had his "big success"? Would he have exposed him? He found he no longer cared. His thoughts were on Lilo. He watched the doctor's back as he bent over her, wondering what was happening, wondering if he should ask; but would he want to know the answer?

194

The ambulance took them to a hospital in the centre of the city. They kept Spencer in Casualty and the last he saw of Lilo was on the stretcher being wheeled away towards the emergency theatre, a doctor hurrying beside her holding the drip.

His own wound was less serious than they had thought. The bullet had passed through the muscle just under his shoulder. They patched him up, put his arm in a sling and said he could go. But he stayed in the hospital with Hoest. They sat in a corridor waiting for news. They sat for a long time without talking, for there was nothing to say now.

A doctor finally came to them. He began to speak to Hoest.

"How is she?" Spencer said, breaking in.

"It is too early to say. The bullet is against her spine."

Abruptly he blurted out, "I want her to get the best. I'll pay. Don't worry about the money."

They looked at him in distaste. The doctor said, "Our medical care here in Germany does not depend on what you can pay."

"Come," Hoest said, and put his hand on Spencer's arm and led him away.

They went out into the bitter evening. "What are you going to do?" Hoest said.

He shrugged. "I don't know."

"Go back home. Try and forget. I know it is hard, but it is the best way." He held up a hand to call his car. "We will drop you at your hotel."

Spencer shook his head and, without saying anything further, turned and walked away along the pavement. His arm was throbbing, and he was feeling the pain. In a strange way it seemed to clear the muddiness from his mind and also it was something he could share with Lilo.

Before he had walked half a mile his thoughts were probing at the future. He had told Hoest he did not know what he was going to do. But he did know. He was going to wait. And every day he was going to visit the hospital. And he was going to her apartment. And he was going to find out where her mother lived. And he was going to see the child . . .

195

He began to walk a little faster. He went round the Breit-scheidplatz in Budapesterstrasse. This was the way he had often walked in the past with Bruno. But the past was gone. He walked on, a pale-faced man with his arm in a sling, utterly alone in the early evening crowd.

*    *    *